MW00425457

DROP

SECRETS
OF
THE HEART

A River of Dreams
Romance

Other books by Heather S. Webber:

The River of Dreams Series
Surrender, My Love

SECRETS
OF
THE HEART

•

Heather S. Webber

AVALON BOOKS
NEW YORK

© Copyright 2003 by Heather S. Webber
Library of Congress Catalog Card Number: 2003090550
ISBN 0-8034-9607-9
All rights reserved.
All the characters in this book are fictitious,
and any resemblance to actual persons,
living or dead, is purely coincidental.
Published by Thomas Bouregy & Co., Inc.
160 Madison Avenue, New York, NY 10016

PRINTED IN THE UNITED STATES OF AMERICA
ON ACID-FREE PAPER
BY HADDON CRAFTSMEN, BLOOMSBURG, PENNSYLVANIA

For Tommy, J.J., & Jackie
All my love.

Chapter One

"In the name of all things holy it is imperative that they be stopped." She poked her cane in his direction. "And you, sir, are just the man to do it."

Reverend John Hewitt rolled his eyes at Mrs. Farrell's use of the word 'holy.' It seemed to greatly differ from his. He guided her to a pew and sat her down. By the look of her flushed face and erratic breathing, it was obvious she needed to rest. "Mrs. Farrell, the Parkers are doing no wrong."

"No wrong," she sputtered. "Why, why they're building a—a—" She apparently struggled to find the right word. "A floating Gomorrah is what they're building." She banged her cane on the polished wood floor for emphasis.

He'd only known the Parkers for a little over a month, but he felt sure enough about their characters to defend them. "Nonsense. They're building a showboat, a floating hotel as I hear told. Elegant accommodations and wholesome family entertainment. There's nothing immoral about that."

"Hearing you say such things makes me question your morals, Reverend," she said haughtily.

1

Her rebuke stung, though he hid it behind passive eyes. He'd given up everything for this job, despite warnings from his superiors that this particular appointment would be trying. And trying it was. The people of River Glen on a whole were anything but conventional and downright misguided. Which only proved to him that he'd made the right decision in coming. They needed him. His guidance.

Even when they couldn't recognize that truth themselves.

Like now.

"Mrs. Farrell, I understand your concern," he began, but was cut off.

"Do you? There will be gambling aboard that steamboat of theirs, imbibing! And just yesterday I heard that those Parker girls are going to be hiring a songstress, no doubt a siren of questionable upbringing if she were to take a position aboard such a blight of society."

"The Parkers are not girls, but sincere young women who wish to fulfill their father's dream—a dream, I daresay, that has become their own since his death."

She huffed. "Women I know do not dress in such a manner. So inappropriate. They don't even have the decency to don a dress while worshipping in God's house."

He was the first to admit that the Parkers were slightly unconventional; that didn't surprise him in the least. Not when it seemed everyone who resided in this town had one odd quirk or another.

What did surprise him was his congregation's dislike of the Parker family. Where his flock could overlook the peculiarities of their close friends, they shunned the Parkers to a degree that embarrassed him whenever he witnessed it firsthand. So he had made it his first unofficial mission: He would, eventually, get through to these misguided souls that their notions of right and wrong had somehow been twisted when in reference to one certain family.

He took a deep breath. "I daresay that God cares more

about their presence than what they are wearing. I do not hear any complaints when Social Leehorn comes to services barefoot and smelling of the pigs he raises."

Mrs. Farrell shifted uncomfortably. "You speak of apples and oranges. Baring one's foot is in no way comparable to baring one's legs."

He bit back a smile. "I have yet to see any one of the Parker women's legs." Unbidden, his thoughts conjured an image of Lou Parker, with her angelic looks and sweet smile, barelegged. He coughed, banishing the image, yet somehow knowing it would return if he chose to let it.

"Their trousers cling in a most—" Her cheeks reddened. "That is to say—" She pursed her lips, clasping her thick arms across her large chest. "It's wrong, Reverend. Sinful. They should be cast out of this church once and for all."

John rubbed his temples in frustration. There was no point in arguing with the old woman. Mrs. Farrell was positive she was right and there was no convincing her otherwise.

The Parkers had been pariahs in River Glen since birth. Their father, popular judge Hiram Parker, had been an eccentric reformer who taught his daughters to be strong, independent. And in this small town those particular traits deemed them wicked.

He thought about that for a moment and decided it wasn't just small towns that shunned the different. He had come from a large city and had experienced the same sort of narrow-mindedness. Only his experience had come from inside his family.

He plucked the cover of a hymnal and said softly, "While I am in charge of this congregation there shall be no casting out. The Parkers have not sinned, and if they had that is a matter between them and God. Not you, or I."

"What of this boat, Reverend? What if it is simply a cover for more . . . lurid activities?"

"Nonsense. Have you forgotten that Alex Parker is wed now to Matthew Kinkade?"

She harrumphed. "Also a man with a questionable background." She leaned forward, her eyes lit with purpose. "I heard a rumor he murdered a man. Do you think it bears merit?"

"I think, Mrs. Farrell, that gossipping is appalling."

She didn't look abashed in the least. "Nevertheless, I am convinced there are scandalous things happening on that steamboat."

To appease her, he said, "What is it, Mrs. Farrell, that you wish me to do?" Not that he had any intention of doing it. His congregation, as much as it pained him to admit, was wrong. They barely knew the Parkers. Not a one had ever taken the time to form a friendship with any of the girls—not after their mother Grace died years ago when they could have used female companionship, and not after their father's death earlier this year when they were left penniless and without a home. That, in his opinion, was the true sin.

"I was hoping you would speak to them, perhaps. Show them the error of their ways, perhaps *befriend* them as part of a master plan to finally be rid of them once and for all."

Sunbeams burst through the stained glass windows, setting the pews alight in color. He judged that it was closing in on two o'clock by the position of the light.

"I don't think so, Mrs. Farrell."

He was running late, yet he sat down. He didn't want Mrs. Farrell to think he was rushing her. After all, it was his job to listen to her even if he didn't agree with what she said.

"I'm not sure how to go about it yet, Reverend Hewitt," she continued on, "but when I figure it out, you'll be the first to know."

He smiled a noncommittal smile and prayed this problem

would wash over soon. The Parkers had been through so much in their lives; they didn't need the added stress of having to deal with his prejudicial congregation.

Helping Mrs. Farrell to the door, he bid her good day and watched as she hobbled down the walkway, her head held high, her fist tightly clenched around her cane.

He quickly walked up the aisle toward the altar, his mind taking in details of the small church even while he was pulling his watch from its pocket in his vest. The floor was clean, the windows clear. Hymnals sat at the end of every pew, and the altar was spotless and ready for his next sermon.

This church had become his salvation, his home since the little family he had was lost to him. Like them or not, his congregation was now all he had. And he'd never do anything to risk losing his position in this church.

He decided he'd alter his sermon from the evils of gossip to one about acceptance. Perhaps, one of these days, his congregation would actually hear it.

His watch, a long-ago gift from his grandmother, clicked as he opened it. The gold was tarnished, its engravings barely visible. Twenty past two. In his small office behind the altar, he removed his white collar and black shirt, and slipped his arms into a shirt of faded blue linen.

A few years back his shirt would have been made from silk, but that was yet another thing he had left behind. In truth, he preferred the linen since it lay cooler on the skin, and the temperatures this late April day climbed with each hour.

His gaze swept over his desk, his Bible. He picked up a sheaf of papers and tucked them into his pocket. Later that night he'd put the finishing touches on his sermon.

From the top of the desk, he lifted an envelope that had arrived the day before. It bore no mark as to who had sent it, yet he knew the sender by the sharp angles of the penmanship.

He took hold of his letter opener, then laid it down again. Still sealed, the envelope was tucked into his pocket next to his sermon. His grandmother's usual pleas for him to return home to New York would have to wait until he was in better spirits.

Locking the back door behind him, he thought again of Mrs. Farrell. If she had any say in the community, he was going to be dragged under by the force of her convictions.

He unbuttoned his top button as the sun beat down, and he silently vowed to buy a hat soon. Though the shops along Main Street had many to choose from, he had trouble parting with his hard-earned money on an item that wasn't a necessity.

Using a shortcut to the heart of town, he met a familiar face on the way. He bent down to rub the dog's head. "I wondered where you'd gotten off to."

The dog had appeared soon after John arrived in River Glen, showing its dirty face at the back of the church whenever John opened the door. After a time it became clear the animal had no owner, so he had taken him in. It had been three months now.

He slapped his thigh. "Come on. We're late."

As he walked down the path the dog kept up, even trotting ahead, already aware of the destination. The path emerged at the rear of Hannah O'Grady's family restaurant. The dog—which he'd yet to call something other than "Dog" because it refused to answer to anything else—trotted over to the back door and barked sharply.

Hannah herself appeared. "You're running late, Reverend," she scolded. "You'll be in trouble for sure."

He watched as she tossed a handful of scraps to Dog. "I know."

She came down the steps. "Does he ever get full?"

John shook his head. "I've yet to see it." He noticed how she wrung her hands together, and waited, knowing she had something more to say. He had known it since she came down off the back stoop of the restaurant.

She glanced up, squinting against the sun. "Mrs. Farrell was in earlier."

Inwardly, he cringed. "I spoke with her this afternoon myself."

"So you know what she's planning . . ."

Puzzled, he folded his arms across his chest. "Planning?"

Her cheeks colored. "I've lived here my whole life, Reverend, and I know most everyone here. I've never held a grudge against no one and that includes the Parkers."

A hint of dread stroked his back. "What *is* being planned, Hannah?"

Dog ambled over, sat at his feet, and growled, as he did at everyone who came within a two-foot radius.

Hannah ignored the mutt. "Nothing yet, Reverend. But sure as I'm standing here, there's trouble on the wind."

"Thanks for the warning, Hannah."

She clambered up the steps. "Sure thing, Reverend."

What could they do? he wondered. Surely nothing extreme or malicious. Though his congregation had their faults, they also had their limits. He just wished he knew what they had in mind, so he could plan to stop it before it got out of hand.

Dog's nails clicked on the cobblestone street as they headed toward the far end of town. A hat in the millinery store caught his eye until he saw the price tag hanging off the brim. He shook his head and pushed on.

How easily he had taken for granted the money of his youth. It had been difficult to forsake, but he had. Difficult, yes, but necessary for his peace of mind. Some things money couldn't buy, like pride.

Levi Mason leaned against the brick wall of his barbershop, sharpening his shears on a chunk of steel. "Clock's a'tickin', Reverend. You're late."

"Indeed I am, Levi."

Stoop-shouldered and eagle-eyed, Levi was one of the oldest residents of River Glen. John came closer, because even though the man could spot a gnat at fifty paces, his hearing was slowly deteriorating.

Dog growled. Levi growled back, and Dog ever so subtly hid behind John's leg.

"They ain't goin' to like you bein' late again."

"They're sure to punish me in their own wicked ways." Indeed, he still ached from the last time he had been late.

Levi shuffled back into his store, a cowbell dinging loudly as he pushed open the door. "I'll be sayin' a prayer for you then."

John looked down the street toward his destination. Dog growled.

"I'll be needing one."

To tell or not to tell, to lie or not to lie.

Many times Lou Parker had tried to cross lying off her list of options, yet somehow it had always worked its way back on.

She worried her lip. Perhaps, since her destination was to see Reverend Hewitt, she should concentrate especially hard on honesty.

Her excursion to see the man could in fact be termed noble.

Oh.

Once again she'd done it. Lied. Even to herself she lied. There was no hope for it, she deemed.

She blew out a small puff of air and looked at the clothing she'd laid out on the bed. It wasn't as though her lying hurt anyone. In fact, hadn't it been she, LouEllen Winifred Parker, who had expedited the marriage of Alex and Matt?

If she hadn't had told her new brother-in-law that small lie about Alex liking him they might not be partaking in the happy marriage they had today.

In retrospect, she ought to be thanked.

Thanked for her lies.

Indeed.

Oh.

There she was, lying yet again. Although she did have a small role in her sister's marriage, it had been love—true, pure love—that had sealed her sister's fate.

Nothing to do with her lies at all.

She picked up a pair of green trousers and held them up to her waist. They seemed too . . . too pea soup. She tossed them back on the bed.

Hammering somewhere beyond her door caught her attention for a moment.

The *Amazing Grace*, her family's steamboat named for her late mother, had been under construction for weeks now. Lou and her sisters had inherited the boat after their father's death, and were now turning the out-of-date freight packet into a floating hotel. Hammering was nothing unusual.

Yet again she pulled her lip into her mouth. Held it there. Nibbled, even. It was almost as bad a habit as lying, yet she couldn't help herself on either front.

The red?

She eyed the pants in question and dismissed them as a choice almost immediately. One did not wear red when meeting with a reverend alone. Certainly not the first time, at the very least.

Her gaze lit on the yellow pair. Daffodil yellow. Several years old, to be sure, but still as bright as the midday sun— as bright, some would say, as her personality.

Another lie.

But they would do. She slipped into them and found a

white blouse trimmed in delicate lace and eased her arms into it.

She looked into the mirror. Turned sideways, backways, and frontways again. Respectable. It had been the image for which she'd been striving. With a quick twist of her wrist and the help of a few pins, she manipulated her hair into a tidy bun.

Infinitely respectable, she decided, despite the trousers.

Glancing at the small clock on her bedside table, she noted the time. If she wanted to see Reverend Hewitt today, she needed to be on her way. Although temperatures felt like summer, it was still spring and darkness fell early.

She cracked open the door.

To tell or not to tell, to lie or not to lie.

She should, at the very least, inform someone she was leaving the boat. Yet . . .

If she told, she'd be asked questions. Pesky questions. Where are you going? What are you doing? Why must you go alone? It was easy enough to sneak away, to avoid the annoyance altogether, but she couldn't. If her absence was noted, her sisters would be frantic, especially after all they'd been through in the last few months with Alex's near death at the hands of a madman.

Her steps were soundless as she walked down the enclosed hallway. The wide bank of windows gleamed from a fresh cleaning and revealed a beautiful spring day, the sun reflecting off the Ohio River.

She couldn't help but peek in on the progress of the Gentlemen's Lounge. Workmen were currently constructing the stage. With a smile on her face, she could easily imagine the lively musical shows she would direct, the songstress seducing a crowd, and the dramatic theater performances.

With a tap on his shoulder, she interrupted the work of

a man hanging wall sconces. "Too high," she told him. She smiled as he lowered it. "Thank you."

The Gentlemen's Lounge was her idea and completely under her control. Matt and Alex had given her free rein and had been overly generous with financing.

Pleased that everything was taking shape, she backtracked down the hall and headed toward the gaming room, or where the gaming room would be once completed. She'd find Jack there, and tell her sister she was off on a mission in the city. Of her two sisters, Jack would be the one to ask the least amount of questions, the one who understood the necessity to escape once in a while.

The pounding of hammers and the humming of saws rhythmically cutting through wood increasingly became louder. Particles of sawdust floated through the air.

Lou stepped into the cavernous room and searched for her sister's long dark hair, a lighthouse in this sea of commotion.

Unable to find her at first glance, she stepped further in. "Miss Parker?"

Lou jumped as a heavy hand touched her arm. Her breath caught, held. Fear whirled through her blood. She spun around. "Mr. Burnett. Hank," she corrected automatically after he'd bid her to call him by his first name at least a dozen times. She breathed in relief. "Hello."

He pulled his hand away quickly, as if regretting having touched her. "Pardon me for saying so, Miss Parker, but you look lost."

Despite his size, he was a gentle man. She told herself to relax; she had nothing to fear from Hank Burnett. Still, a month after the incident with Alex, apprehension lingered as Lou remembered the evil man who had tried to kill her sister. She pushed the images out of her head. There was nothing he could do to harm her family now, as he was locked in a jail in New Orleans for life.

"Not quite lost, no," she said to Hank. "But on a mission."

Hank Burnett had proved himself a hard worker, and she considered him a friend. He was odd, to be sure, but since he was born and raised in River Glen, he fit right in.

Although she'd known Hank Burnett for nigh on twenty years now, he insisted upon calling her Miss Parker at all times, even though he was less formal with her sisters.

Confusion dipped his eyebrows into a hairy V. "A mission, Miss Parker?"

A hammer rested in his belt loop. His large hands were clean but callused as he clenched and unclenched his fists. Lou took in the way he wouldn't look at her, the way he bounced ever so slightly on the balls of his feet, and tried to put the man at ease. "I'm looking for my sister, Hank. Has she given directives, then abandoned ship?" she teased.

His gaze turned dark. "Oh no. Miss Jack, she went to fetch some water."

Lou almost explained that she had been joshing but he looked too serious. She feared clarification might hurt his feelings.

"She should be right back," he said.

She looked up at Hank, for she looked up at most everybody, and realized he was a solution to her problem. She could tell him she was off on an errand—that was the truth—and she wouldn't have to face any questions at all.

Linking her arm through his, she gazed up with a smile meant to charm. "Perhaps you can do me an act of kindness?"

He stared at her hand resting on his forearm. "Yes'm."

A niggle of doubt worked its way into her conscience. She released his arm and clasped her hands behind her back. "Might you tell Jack when she returns that I've set out on an errand?"

He cast a sharp gaze to the wide bank of tall narrow

windows that permitted a view of the Public Landing. "Alone?"

To lie or not to lie. If she said she would be alone, he'd want to escort her, being the gentleman he was, and that simply was not an option she dared consider. If she told him she had accompaniment, she'd be lying. Yet again.

"Lou?"

She turned to find Jack coming into the room, a bucket of water in one hand. Lou suspected many a man in the room cringed at the sight, and had most likely offered assistance only to receive a scolding in return. Jack was fiercely independent.

"Are you off somewhere?" her sister asked, eyeing Lou's riding boots.

Lou looked between Hank and Jack. Somehow she sensed it would be easier to lie to her sister. "Thank you, Hank. I'll tell her myself."

He tipped his head, his gold hair speckled with sawdust. "Yes'm."

Lou motioned Jack into the enclosed hallway of the Texas Deck, the second level of the boat. Pounding resonated off the leaded windows. "I'm going out for a while."

"So I see. Where?"

"Out is all."

"Where?"

Lou took a deep breath and held it as she tried to rein in her temper. All her life she'd had to answer to someone. "To River Glen."

"Whatever for?"

"I need to speak with someone."

A smile curved Jack's lips. "A holy someone?"

To lie. Unquestionably to lie. "I'm not certain of what you're speaking."

Jack laughed. "It's most obvious when you're near him that you're smitten with the good reverend."

Lou faked shock. "How obscene. He's a man of God!"

Her sister continued to laugh. Indeed, tears came to her eyes. "You fool many a person, Lou, but you can't fool me. He is a man of God. A human man of God, a quite handsome man of God, a man of God who is allowed to wed."

Tightly, Lou said, "I'll be back before nightfall."

"Take a hack. Don't ride alone."

She heard the worry in Jack's voice. Apparently her sister still harbored fears of her own after all they went through in New Orleans. Lou allowed this one concession. "I will."

She hurried down the steps to the cargo hold, which now bore an amazing resemblance to a hotel foyer, and rushed down the stage onto the solid ground of the Landing.

Holding to her word, she headed to the livery where she hired a hack to drive her the four miles to River Glen. And when she discovered the reverend was neither home, nor at his church, she'd smiled sweetly at the driver and asked him to stop at Hannah O'Grady's restaurant to see if Hannah knew where the reverend might be found.

She'd have asked herself, but feared people would simply look through her, as they always did.

Almost always, she amended, waiting for the driver to return.

Reverend John Hewitt looked at her. Looked at her as if he cared.

The driver ambled out of the restaurant, a piece of pie in one hand.

"Did she know?" Lou asked.

"Yes ma'am."

"Can you take me there?"

He nodded and climbed into his seat. A few moments later he reined in the horses.

Lou stepped out of the hired carriage, paid the driver.

"Should I wait?"

She nibbled her lip. "No. No thank you."

He tipped his head sharply, set the horses into a trot.

Lou kept to the tree line behind the school as she inched closer to the reverend and his flock, listening to what appeared to be a heated conversation.

"But that means we're a man short," Hex Goolens shouted. He tossed his wooden bat on the ground.

Reverend Hewitt shook his head, his dark hair slightly matted to his forehead. A mangy dog sat at his feet, growling low in its throat. "You know the rules, Hex."

"Awww, Reverend." A dirty leather ball joined the bat on the ground.

To Hex, he said, "Temper, temper." He turned to all gathered. "I'm sorry, boys. We're going to have to cancel today's game."

Lou watched for a second as the Reverend crouched down to talk to a smaller boy. His broad shoulders stretched the fabric of his shirt taut as he reached out and rubbed the child's head.

As John rose to his feet, Lou stepped out of the woods. She walked calmly over to the group, even though their open stares made her want to retreat. She ignored the growling of the dog that'd risen at her approach and cleared her throat. Her heartbeat pounded against her ribcage. "I'll be your ninth man, Reverend."

Chapter Two

"Y ou?" Hex Goolens fell to the ground, laughing.

Lou ignored him. She noticed that the other boys all wore expressions of interest mingled with unease. She ignored them too.

"You know how to play baseball, Miss Parker?" the reverend asked.

"Indeed."

She couldn't read his thoughts as he stared above her head. Would he send her away? She clenched her fists and waited.

He pushed a hand through his shaggy brown hair, then settled it on a tapered waist. "I cannot see why she shouldn't play."

Hex stopped laughing, scrambled to his knees. "But she's a girl!" he protested.

The reverend looked her over. "Quite."

Heat spilled into her cheeks, but she remained silent. John Hewitt's eyes had yet to release her gaze. The hue of his eye was blue, so unlike hers that she could scarce believe the two could be termed the same color. His was the blue of early night, of the darkest sapphire.

She didn't dare look away. This was the first opportunity to see him out of his clerical clothes. Here, out in this field, surrounded by boys, a dog at his feet, he hardly looked reverent. Yet, it was there. In the depths of his eyes. His serenity shone bright, along with his wisdom and quiet strength.

"I don't wanna play with no girl." Hex climbed to his feet, towering over her.

She forced her gaze from the reverend and turned to the boy. To show fear is a weakness, her father had often said. Not that she was afraid Hex would harm her physically. No, the pain he would inflict would be internal. One would think she'd have grown accustomed to it after awhile. Unfortunately, she'd yet to learn how to keep words from hurting.

"Then we won't play." Reverend John Hewitt gathered the bat and ball and shoved them into Hex's arms.

Lou studied the boy. Eleven, perhaps twelve, he was tall and lanky, and obviously used to getting his way if the set to his chin and the pout of his lip were any indication.

Through the household gossip, Lou remembered hearing of his birth simply because of his unusual name. After the birth of Mrs. Goolens's ninth child, Doc Steiner had apparently told her that she would be unable to have more children, which had been quite a relief to the poor woman. Two months later she was expecting yet again and claimed the doctor had hexed her.

And the people in this small town thought her family odd?

Hex flashed an angry glare her way. "I don't want *her* on my team."

"Reverend Hewitt?"

Lou turned to the voice. A younger boy she didn't recognize scuffed his feet on the grass, his eyes intent on her face as if she were the devil himself. He said, "I'm not sure my mama would want me to play with . . . with her."

A wound that had festered for many years broke open inside Lou's soul. Her stomach tightened as if being bound with rope. She hoped her pain didn't show on her face. It usually didn't, not that many people ever looked for it.

She met the reverend's gaze and looked away quite quickly, turning her attention to the mutt that seemed attached to John Hewitt's shoes. The dog looked up, saw her, and growled.

Her focus shifted once again, diverted as the reverend bent down to the child's eye level. "Have you ever met Miss Parker, Harry?" he said, his tone soft but firm.

The boy shook his head, unruly locks of blond covering his eyes.

The reverend stood. "Boys, this is Miss Lou Parker. She has lived in River Glen near her whole life. I urge you, strongly, to disregard anything you may have heard and judge her for yourselves."

Lou watched him closely as he spoke. His face shone with conviction. She was pleased that he didn't try to cover the fact that most of these children had heard the gossip of their parents, and for the older ones, had probably partaken in some of it themselves. He wanted these boys to form their own opinions, despite what they might have heard. Which, she speculated, was quite a lot.

A faint glossy sheen shone on the reverend's forehead, and his linen shirt clung to his back, outlining the muscles beneath the fabric. He turned to her. "Would you care to say anything, Miss Parker?"

Nervousness produced a lump in her throat. She swallowed hard, trying to dislodge it. She had trouble speaking in front of large groups of people, even if those people were bedraggled children. She cleared her throat. "Please, please, call me Lou. Miss Parker is much too schoolmarmish."

A few boys smiled. The weight in her chest shifted, ever so slightly. She wondered if she should say something to defend her reputation. No, she wouldn't. She'd let these boys decide for themselves whether or not they liked her.

"But Reverend," young Harry said. "My mama."

The reverend ruffled the boy's hair. "Let me worry about your mama. You won't be in trouble for simply playing a game."

The boy looked doubtful but nodded.

"Can you play?" one of the older boys asked Lou, hands on hips.

She nodded.

"Hah!" Hex exclaimed, earning him a stern look from John Hewitt.

"A contest, then?" Lou offered.

The cocky look in the boy's eyes faltered for a second, but his bravado soon took hold. "What kind?"

"Miss Parker, I don't know—"

"Lou," she told the reverend resolutely. "Call me Lou." She then spoke quickly before the reverend could utter another word, effectively cutting off his protestations. "Hex and I, his bat against my pitch."

A whoop went through the crowd. The dog rose to its haunches and looked around as if it had missed something important.

"If I strike him out," Lou said, "I am allowed to play. Today and all days I can make the games."

Hex stepped toward her, his brown eyes interested. "And if you don't?"

He said it in a manner that raised her hackles. As if she *couldn't*. Whether he thought so because she was a Parker, or merely a girl, she couldn't be sure.

"If I don't strike you out, then I will see to it that everyone here receives two tickets to a Cincinnati Reds game at Redland Field."

There was a bit of stunned silence before joyous hollers sent the birds from the trees, shattering the stillness of the spring afternoon.

"Miss Parker—"

She narrowed her eyes on John Hewitt.

"I mean, Lou." He raised his voice to be heard over the boys, who obviously thought they had won before the competition had even begun. "That's a pricey bargain."

She tipped her head to the side, her eyes widened, a smile teasing her lips upward. "Have you no faith, Reverend?"

His eyes rounded in shock just before his lips curved into a grin that nearly stole her breath. He waved an arm toward the makeshift playing field. "Let's have at it, then."

"Might I borrow your glove?" she asked him.

He handed it to her. "Consider it yours."

Hex tossed her the ball. She fumbled it, and it plunked to the ground. Laughter singed her ears. She smiled inwardly as she bent to pick the ball up. When she rose, she caught a look from the reverend.

It was a sideways look, contemplative. Assessing. The edge of his upper lip jerked slightly, and she thought that he was trying hard to suppress a smile.

Clearly, he suspected she'd dropped the ball on purpose. He was right, but how did he know?

He is a man of God, she told herself, more curious than guilty. She stepped up to the homemade pitcher's mound, a chunk of whitewashed wood.

Hex stood at home plate, bending slightly forward, the bat poised over his right shoulder. His eyes had lost any element of youth and playfulness and had taken on a look of serious intent.

She rolled her shoulders to loosen them while carefully watching the crowd. A ripple of fear shot up her back. She forced it away. They were but children. And she was not singing. This was an entirely different matter.

She stood with her legs apart and rapidly swung her arm back, then forward again, completing a backwards circle in the blink of an eye. She stepped forward and released the ball as her arm finished the second rotation. The ball sailed over Hex's head.

The boys laughed, and she definitely heard one compare her to a rabid whirligig.

"Oops," she said.

She didn't dare look at the reverend. She had the uneasy feeling he knew what she was up to.

Someone tossed the ball back to her. She dropped it again, and slowly bent to pick it up.

Perhaps she shouldn't drag this out, she thought. Yet she was having fun. She couldn't remember the last time she'd had this much fun.

Fun at the boys' expense, she reminded herself. Guilt trickled into her conscience. And when she wound up again, she took the matter seriously.

The ball flew over home plate and landed smack dab in the center of Baxter Wed's homemade catcher's glove, knocking him off balance.

"Strike one," she heard the reverend say. Quite clearly too, for all the boys had gone slack-jawed, rendered silent.

The catcher threw the ball back to her, and she snatched it out of the air, pulling it close to her chest. She heard a few whispered 'ahhhs.'

Looking between the catcher's glove and Hex's determined expression, she debated where to put the ball. High or low?

Low.

She threw it, and Hex swung. The crack of the bat echoed as the ball flew behind Hex, into the woods.

"Strike two."

She heard nothing in the reverend's voice that told her of how he was feeling. It occurred to her that he would want to remain neutral, but selfishly, she supposed, she wanted someone cheering for her.

The sun dipped behind darkening clouds as Baxter again tossed the retrieved ball back to her. Hex's hair lay flat on his head. Perspiration dampened his brow. He dragged his bat across the plate and took a few practice swings. He nodded to her when he was ready.

She threw the ball; he swung, losing his balance as the ball landed with a soft thud into the catcher's mitt.

"Strike three."

Lou looked around for a moment, at the blank faces. She'd guaranteed her place on the team, but had she made enemies of all these boys?

All at once a loud cheer went up, and the boys ran over to her, asking her what seemed like a million questions. But it was Hex she watched closely.

He dusted himself off and walked over to her. She held her head high, waiting. Waiting to hear him repeat some of the terrible things she'd heard all her life, simply because she was different.

To her amazement, he smiled. "Want to be on my team?"

She glanced at the reverend, who looked as shocked as she felt.

"I'd love to."

The corner of John's mouth hitched, but he said nothing as Lou walked away, Hex at her side. This lot might not be the most refined, but for the most part, they'd been raised with a firm hand and a strong sense of right and wrong.

Hex's acceptance of Lou was a good sign things could change. John hoped it was possible for his congregation to open their minds as these children had. But he feared it would take more than an uncanny pitching ability to change the mentality of the elders in town.

"Batter up," he yelled.

Baxter Wed stepped up to the plate. He swung on the first pitch and knocked the ball deep into the field.

John covered first base, and as Baxter rounded it, he shoved John out of the way, knocking him over. "Hey!" John called out.

He could see Baxter's smirk as he settled himself at third base. "Sorry, Reverend. The nature of the game and all."

John bit back a laugh. The game. Hah! He'd been late and now he knew his penance.

He looked around for Dog, realizing for the first time that he wasn't at his usual post by John's foot. John's mouth dropped ever so slightly as he spotted Dog curled in front of Lou Parker. If the dog were a cat, John had no doubt he'd have been purring from the gentle rubbing Lou was administering to his ears.

For a moment, a brief moment, John imagined Lou's hands on his own neck, rubbing tenderly away the knots that formed there each night.

A gust of wind brought him out of his daydream. Leaves rustled as he tried to keep his focus on the game.

There were two outs when little five-year-old Tommy Beasley stepped up to the plate. John nearly laughed. The bat was almost as big as the boy.

At his position at first base, John yelled, "How many outs does your team have, Tommy?"

"Two," the little guy called out.

"How many are you allowed?"

"Three."

John noticed Lou watching him. It sent something warm through his veins he didn't dare try to identify.

"How many more does our team need? Three take away two."

He could see Tommy struggling to do the math. The boy balanced the bat under one arm and used stubby fingers to subtract. A toothless grin winked at him as he said, "One!"

"Good job."

"And it's not gonna be me," he said, swinging. The ball dribbled in front of home plate. Tommy ran as fast as his tiny legs would carry him, finally reaching base. Where he promptly shoved John backward, into the grass.

Lou's musical laughter carried on the air. John pushed himself to his feet and glanced her way. She sat on the grass next to Hex and Baxter, turning her head between one and the other. He couldn't hear what they asked her, but he hoped to the heavens above they were being tactful.

She plucked at a strand of grass and looked toward him, her shyness evident in the tilt of her head, the bashful look beneath her pale lashes. She caught him staring and looked away, clapping as Collier Dennison took aim at the baseball.

John knew he ought to be paying attention, but he couldn't keep his gaze from Lou. Lou. There was much he didn't know about her. All this time he had thought her shy and quiet, yet here she presented another side of herself.

How much courage, he wondered, had it taken for her to invite herself to play a game of baseball? And as for quiet, she seemed to be the one doing the most cheering for her team.

Which side represented the real woman?

Collier struck out, and the teams switched positions. Dog raised a sleepy eyelid and thumped his tail as John knelt in the grass beside him.

Darkening clouds shaded the field. Just as Lou pitched her first ball, a fat raindrop splashed John's nose. A bolt of lightning lit the sky to the west, and thunder rumbled in the distance.

"Take cover!" John shouted. The boys scattered.

Lou ran over to him, her cheeks pink, aglow with good health. "How fun! Do you always incorporate the math lesson?"

"It keeps them focused in school. If they get a bad grade, they aren't allowed to play."

"It's a good thing I came along then." She smiled serenely. "I have a way with numbers."

"You have a way with a ball too. That was an unusual style of pitching."

"Being so small, I need the momentum of the circles for a faster pitch."

Droplets of rain multiplied into a soaking shower, and he took her elbow and ran for the shelter of the schoolhouse.

Glancing around he said, "Where's your carriage?"

"I don't have one."

"How did you get here?" He yelled to be heard above the rumbling of thunder. He tugged on the doors to the schoolhouse only to find them locked.

"I took a hack."

Rain dripped off her nose. Wisps of blond hair molded her face. She spun in a circle, holding her hands up to cup the rain as it fell. "Isn't this wonderful?"

Her laughter echoed, stirring something inside him, bringing it to life. The look of pleasure in her eyes was one he'd never forget. The amazing violet-colored orbs radiated happiness.

He laughed. "It's something. Let me take you to the livery to find you a ride home."

Her smile faltered. She grabbed his arm. "Oh no. I can't go back."

Thunder boomed. "Why not?"

She pushed a thoroughly soaked lock of hair from her

line of vision. "Because I came to River Glen to speak with you, Reverend."

He looked down as Dog growled, and his gaze skipped over Lou. It was only then that he noticed her shirt. Soaked through with rain, the white had become translucent, revealing the seams of the camisole she wore beneath. And more. Much more.

He swallowed hard and forced his gaze away. She had yet to notice the state of her appearance as she raised her face upward, letting the rain spill across her features.

Lord help him.

"To speak with me?" he said, inanely.

"Yes."

He wouldn't look at her, and he couldn't take her to the church, not in her present . . . condition. It was too risky. Although nothing improper was taking place, tongues would wag, and her reputation would be beyond repair . . . and his would be ruined as well. "I think it's, uh, best, then if I take you home."

"But I said I couldn't go—"

He clarified. "To my home."

He saw the flash of emotion cross her features before she reined it in and immediately suspected she did that quite often. When he suggested they go back to his house, he should have known better. After all, his home had once been hers. What kind of memories would going back there bring out?

Lightning lit the sky. "That—that'll be perfect," she said, her voice soft. "For I have a favor of the utmost importance to ask of you."

Chapter Three

She knew a shortcut. For a month now he'd been trekking from the schoolhouse to his own house, never knowing there was a path through the woods that practically led to his back door.

John pushed that particular door open and ushered her into the kitchen. Dog followed at his heels, shaking the rain from his knotted fur.

As John started a fire in the hearth, he stole glances at Lou, who shivered while looking around, taking in the space. She was soaked through, and her teeth chattered.

He struck a match and held it to the kindling. The fire sparked. He turned back to her, following her gaze, wondering what she thought of his lack of possessions. If the house hadn't been sold at auction for a ridiculously low sum, he never would have been able to afford it. There was little money left to furnish the place.

She caught him staring and looked down, only to look up again a moment later, the shyness back in her violet eyes.

"I'll, uh—" He gestured toward her clothes. "I'll find you something dry to wear."

"Oh!" It was the first time she'd noticed her disrepair. Not his first time, though. He'd tried to keep his gaze fixated anywhere but her, but it kept sliding back to her trim form.

Against his better judgment.

Against his knowing better.

"Thank you," she said in a whisper.

There was a quiet grace about her that impressed him. Earlier he'd seen it when young Harry had unintentionally maligned her character. She had simply lifted that delicate nub of a chin, and schooled her face into an expression of disinterest. He suspected it was a lesson learned long before.

And now here she was, dripping on his flooring, with that same look of quiet grace. Most girls her age would have undoubtedly screamed, fainted, or simpered like a wounded pup. Or, knowing most of the River Glen's female population, done all three.

Lou was no simpering female. Though color had swept across her face, settling into her cheeks and the tips of her ears, she said nothing.

No simpering.

No screaming.

No fainting.

She simply folded her graceful arms across her chest, nibbled her lip, and looked at him.

Looking at her.

He rushed from the room, saying a prayer of penance as he went.

A smile tugged at the corner of Lou's mouth, but she refused to give in to the urge to laugh at the reverend's embarrassment.

Her own was too great.

She pulled at the limp fabric that molded her skin. She

flapped it in front of the fire, hoping it would speed the drying time, but when she released the fabric once more, it adhered to her skin the way a barnacle clung to a tugboat.

Her pants, beyond being drenched, had a multitude of grass stains covering both knees and hems. How was she ever going to explain her appearance to her sisters?

She crossed over to the fire, and was surprised to hear the tapping of paws as John's dog followed behind her. She bent to rub the dog's head, but stopped when it growled.

"You act like a feisty thing, but you don't fool me." She rubbed the dog's ears and its tail thumped in happy rhythm. Its brown eyes seemed truly sad and lonely as it stared up at her. Then it collapsed into a furry ball at her feet, set its head upon its paws, and fell into a quick sleep before the dancing flames.

She could see no outward scars on the dog, but with every growl, she knew its pain. Though she smiled through her own hurt instead of growling, they both had the same wish: for somebody to see through the pretense and give them acceptance and love, simply for who they were.

For the dog, that person was John. Was he also the person for her?

She dismissed the foolish notion immediately. How silly of her to even have thought it in the first place. Or so she told herself.

Truth be told, she liked the reverend. Liked him very much indeed. Too much, perhaps. She sighed. Even if he returned her feelings, and she saw no signs he had such inclinations. A match between them would never work. Not in this town, where gossip and intolerance would always keep them apart.

Sighing, she bent and scratched the dog's head as it slept, her back warming with the heat of the fire. Footsteps thumped across the ceiling in what used to be her parents' bedroom. Of course it would now be the reverend's, seeing that it was the largest room in the house.

Determined not to think of her parents, she cast her hands toward the flames, warming them.

It wasn't, she supposed, the notion of John living here that bothered her so.

It was more that she wasn't.

She'd been born in this house, lost her first tooth in this very room at four, when she fell and banged her mouth on the brick hearth. Every nook in this room, and all the others, were familiar. Each held irreplaceable memories.

Focusing on the fire, she stared into the orange-blue flames and tried not to remember all the times she'd done the same thing before.

She didn't think she'd miss the house. Her older sister Alex was the sentimental one. The one who cared about the notches in the doorframe that charted the sisters' growth. Alex had been the one who'd insisted the house remain in the family after their father's death.

And Alex had been the one who'd had her heart broken when the bank sold the house at auction before the sisters could raise enough money by operating the *Amazing Grace*, their only inheritance, to buy it back.

Lou hadn't realized how much she missed the oversized Victorian until John Hewitt had pushed her through the back door and out of the rain.

"Lou?"

She turned and found the object of her thoughts framed in the doorway, light from the hall spilling across his face.

She bit back a sigh. A more handsome man she'd never seen, with his stubborn chin, autocratic nose, and kind, deep-set eyes. He'd redressed in his official clothes: black pants, black shirt, white collar. "Reverend. I didn't hear you come down." She automatically folded her arms over her chest, though the fabric had dried enough to provide a bit of modesty.

He gave her a stern look. "If I am permitted to call you Lou, you must call me John."

She nodded, secretly pleased. If nothing more, they could be friends. Silently, she hoped that statement true and not another of her small fabrications.

He stepped closer, and she noticed he wouldn't look at her.

Then she remembered why. Embarrassed heat flushed her face.

He thrust a pile of material toward her. "I—these were all I could find."

She took the clothes and pressed them tight against her chest, biting back a smile. His actions were so disjointed and awkward, they cast him in a new light. A light she found utterly appealing. "Thank you. Anything is better than what I have on."

Still gazing at the wall, he said, "You can change in the bathroom. It's down the hall on the right."

She did smile then. "I know."

His eyes closed in a tight wince. "I'm sorry. I forgot."

"No need to apologize . . . John."

She heard pots clattering in the kitchen as she changed. John's shirt hung to her knees, and the trousers he'd given her wouldn't stay up even after she rolled the waist. She abandoned them on the floor.

The shirt was a far cry from respectable but it would have to do, and, she reasoned, it was almost as long as a dress.

Almost.

The shadow of the gilded mirror that once hung above the sink still remained, the mirror long sold at auction to repay some of her late father's debt.

Why hadn't the reverend replaced it? Or, at the very least, applied a coat of paint to the walls?

Perhaps he'd been too busy.

Yes, that must be so.

She smiled. It bolstered her courage to ask the rev—To ask John her favor. For what she was to ask overstepped all bounds of propriety, not that doing so had ever stopped her before. But, somehow, with John, it was different. She was different.

She wanted to please him.

And she didn't know, with her reputation in River Glen, if that was a possibility. How far would he allow their friendship to stretch?

She wasn't a fool. And she wasn't as simple as some might think. Although she often kept them to herself, she had opinions, and she was intelligent.

How long before those children at the baseball game told their parents of her presence? How long until those parents sought John out to reprimand him?

She shook her head, droplets flying. She couldn't dwell on it. Wouldn't. The faults of others were not her own. She couldn't change the people of this town, or their opinion of her family, but she could do all she could to prove to them that they were wrong about her character.

Looking around the water closet, she found a comb in a basket inside the towel hutch.

There was something about this moment . . . being alone with John, wearing his shirt, his comb in her hand.

It was as though she were dreaming.

A knock at the door startled her. "Lou, are you all right in there?"

Not a dream at all. Reality. Sweet reality. Though, she confessed, not all. In her dream, there had been a band of gold on her finger. She nearly laughed aloud at the silent confession. Foolish fantasy.

"Lou?"

"I'm fine," she called out. She heard a mumbled "Good" come through the thick, paneled door.

"Do you want some tea?" he asked.

"Yes." Why were they shouting? Lou stepped toward the door, her feet gliding over the cool oak floorboards. She twisted the knob and John tumbled into the room, knocking her over. Together, they landed in a heap on the floor.

Her breathing ceased as she stared up into his deep blue eyes.

A flicker of something she couldn't identify swept over his features an instant before he met her gaze.

His weight felt oddly comfortable on top of her rather than crushing. She knew she ought to say something, to push him off her. But if she were honest with herself, for a change, she'd admit that she liked where she was just fine.

His blue gaze darkened, his pupils widening. He glanced from her eyes to her lips and up again.

His elbows rested next to her cheeks. One of his legs was caught between hers. Her chest tightened with a need born of her earlier fantasy, squeezing, fighting to be heard.

She let out a rush of air and the spell was broken.

John scrambled off her, swiping a hand through his damp hair as he gained his feet.

He cast a look around the water closet as if to assure himself that they were truly alone. Finally, his gaze landed on her once again.

"Forgive me!" He reached out a hand and pulled her to her feet. "Are you okay? I didn't hurt you, did I?"

Mentally, she checked for pain. Her backside was a bit sore, but she'd eat lye soap before admitting so. "No. I'm quite all right." Absently, she noted that she still held the comb.

His gaze bore into her. "Please accept my apolo—" He looked down.

"What is it?" Her gaze followed his downward. The tails

of his shirt brushed below her knees. She wiggled her toes. Yes, there were ten of them, all present and accounted for.

"Your—" He cleared his throat. "Your legs. They're bare." He cupped his mouth, trying to hide a smile behind his long fingers.

"And that amuses you?" she asked merely out of curiosity, since he seemed to find her lower limbs humorous.

His gaze widened, his smile fled. "Oh, ahem, no. It's just that Mrs. Farrell this afternoon was speaking of your legs . . ."

At the mention of Mrs. Farrell's name Lou went cold. It was no secret what the old woman thought of her and her sisters.

She set her hands on her hips. "Why, may I ask, were my legs a topic of discussion between yourself and Mrs. Farrell?" Anger heated her blood, sent her pulse pounding. "Doesn't she have a multitude of my other flaws to choose from? Surely she could find nothing wrong with my legs."

She lifted the tails of the shirt and stuck her leg out, setting it on the edge of the cast iron bathtub. "It's but a leg. Muscle and bone." She jerked it toward him. "See! See!"

At his shocked expression, she drew in a deep breath. Heat infused her arms, her neck, her cheeks.

Oh.

Goodness.

She smoothed the shirt down, tugging at the tails, wishing it was floor-length. What was she doing? She turned her back on him, not wanting him to see her tears.

She'd just bared her legs to a man of God.

A man of God!

She berated herself for giving in to her temper. Usually she kept it well hidden behind a façade of tranquility.

It must be this town, she thought, sniffling.

This house.

This man.

She'd let her guard down and now he'd seen a part of her few others had.

She heard the creak of the faucet and wished he leave her be. Unfortunately, he apparently had contradictory thoughts. He stepped in front of her and pressed a cool cloth to her face.

She hiccupped. "What's that for?"

"Your face," he said with a gentle smile.

His features were devoid of any judgment, of any censure. On the contrary, his eyes held a bounty of compassion. So much so it made her eyes well once again.

"The cool water helps with the blotches."

Panic raced up her spine. "Blotches?" She cupped her cheeks, and he brushed her hands away.

"It's your coloring. Have you never seen the blotches? My mother had them every time she was upset."

Lou shook her head. Blotches! That's what he saw when he looked at her?

The cloth shifted on her face. "I should have known," he said softly, as he curved the cloth over her cheek and under her chin.

"Known? Known what?"

His blue gaze held her captive. "That you never cry, Lou. That you don't allow yourself to get angry."

She backed away, wrapping her arms around herself. He was too close to opening a wound long left alone.

"Either that," he said, "or you simply don't allow your emotions to surface." He tipped up her chin, looked into her eyes. "Which is it?"

Chapter Four

"It's—" She broke off, not just unwilling but unable to speak of her emotions. They had long been tightly bound within her, and she was not used to acknowledging them, never mind speaking of them.

John placed the cloth on the lip of the sink and turned to face her. "It's what?"

She swallowed. More than anything she wanted to open up to this man, to allow him to see all she was, not just the image she presented to so many. Yet it had been so long since she felt free with her feelings. She hadn't been truly honest with anyone, not even herself since the day—

She shook her head. She would not think about it. That memory best lay dormant. Looking up, she found John staring at her, waiting for her to say something, to reveal her innermost thoughts. She simply couldn't.

Tugging on the tails of her shirt, she said, "Is the tea ready?" She smiled, felt it falter, and put more effort into it.

Most men would have taken the hint that she wanted to be alone—though, she reflected, most men wouldn't have been in this situation in the first place.

She was quickly learning John Hewitt was not like most men.

It seemed she'd known that from their first meeting, hadn't she? There had been something there, between them, the day John presided over the marriage of Alex and Matt. It had been indescribable, the immediate, strong sensation upon meeting him, and it remained electric. It was still there, still in the air, and when he touched her as he often did, through a handshake or a guiding hand on her back, it seeped through her skin, tingling, warming.

He took a step toward her, and she resisted the urge to retreat, though she liked his nearness. She simply didn't want to have a conversation regarding her emotions. Not now. Not ever.

"You don't have to hide from me, Lou," he said gently, his voice resonating within her chest, loosening the restraints on those feelings of failure and unworthiness.

She bit out a laugh, hoping it didn't sound strained. "Me? I have nothing to hide. Every person in River Glen knows everything about me. In fact, I wouldn't be the least surprised if they even knew my shoe size."

"Do they?"

Her brows lifted. "Do they know my shoe size?"

The corner of his lip lifted most enticingly. "You know quite well what I was asking, but if you insist on pretending otherwise, I will ask straight out: Do they know the real you?"

Of course she'd known what he meant. She apparently wasn't as good an actress as she thought she was. How could he see through her so easily? It was a perfectly discomfiting notion.

She tugged at the shirttails yet again and eyed the pair of trousers draped over the side of the tub. She would wear them, drooping or not. Perhaps her hairpins could hold the fabric together if manipulated in just the right—

"Lou."

She jumped. "Yes?"

"You have yet to answer me."

She tipped her head. "I'm quite aware of that fact."

His deep blue gaze narrowed. "I will let the matter be. For now," he added.

"The tea?" she asked sweetly.

He nodded, his gaze never leaving her face. Gone was the look of compassion, replaced now with one of determination. However, she had an iron will, and a lifetime of being able to keep her innermost desires secret. She lifted her chin.

He sighed in temporary defeat and backed out the door, calling over his shoulder, "Sugar or milk?"

"Neither," she answered as she put on John Hewitt's pants. "I like mine strong."

His voice was but a mere echo. "I should have known."

"A rather angry bird told me that the *Amazing Grace* is hiring a singer," John said as he sat down in the chair Lou had dragged over to the fire for him.

To look at her, she seemed so frail—especially in clothes that hung on her—yet she'd proved more than once today that she could hold her own, both mentally and physically.

Lou looked up from her tea, firelight reflected in her violet eyes. "Word travels fast."

"Indeed it does." Where the Parkers were concerned it seemed as though River Glen had a phone line tapped into every household in the community. How people gleaned their information, he did not know.

"It's almost as though the congregation has a spy aboard." She leveled a stern gaze on him. "You wouldn't know anything about that, would you?"

"No," he said honestly, though he suspected the suspicion true. "They know I'd never approve. Tell me about your plans." He rested an ankle atop its opposite knee.

Again she looked at him, her gaze wide. In its depths he could see what she tried so valiantly to hide: She wanted to be accepted, to know that what she said would not be mocked or ridiculed. He wished for her trust, but supposed he'd have to earn it. After all, the people in this town had hurt her so many times before.

Apparently sensing his sincerity, she said, "We're looking for a singer for the Gentlemen's Lounge. She will sing songs. Nothing more. Nothing less."

Dog's ears perked, then flopped, as he dropped back into sleep. Out of the corner of his eye, John noticed Lou's foot rubbing Dog's belly. Something in his chest twisted almost painfully. "Anyone apply as of yet?"

She nibbled her lip. "I have several interviews scheduled for tomorrow. There are professional singers coming from as far as Chicago. They have been impressed by the reputation the *Amazing Grace* is earning through word of mouth for its elegance and style."

John sipped his tea. "Why not take the job yourself?"

He wasn't quite sure how it happened, but he'd offended her in some way. Her face lost all color, and her knuckles whitened as her grip tightened on her teacup. He gently wrested it from her grasp, fearing the thin porcelain would break under the force.

"Lou? Did I say something wrong?"

Dog barked. John absently patted his head as sparks spit from the hearth.

She shook her head. "I don't sing." He saw the transformation in her face, the careful hiding of all emotion before she gave him *that* smile, the one she used when pretending all was fine when it was not. "You're mistaken."

"You have a beautiful voice. I've heard it in church." How could he not? It seemed to him that it rose above all others, leading in not just beauty but true spirit. Surely, she must know of her gift.

She jumped out of her seat and stalked across the kitchen, finally stopping at the bank of windows overlooking the backyard.

The rain was ending, and soon she would be going. A slip of panic pulsed in his veins. When would he see her again? Surely she would be at Sunday services, but that wasn't what he meant. When would he see her again, like this? Without the invisible armor she wore when visiting River Glen? When would he see the joyous smile, the *real* smile, she had given him while standing in the rain outside the schoolhouse? He didn't understand why seeing that smile again was so important to him, but knew it was by the way his heart hammered, his stomach tightened, at the thought of never again seeing the Lou he'd met today.

Softly, her voice carried across the kitchen. "There are others more talented. I will hire one of them."

He let the matter be. He heard the pain in her voice, though he didn't understand it. Perhaps one day she would tell him, confide in him, let him be her friend.

"How are the preparations coming? Is everything on schedule?"

"Yes. Jack has the gaming room in fine form. Alex has completely redecorated all the cabins, and Matt has the route to St. Louis memorized."

"Will all the journeys be to St. Louis and back?"

"No. It will vary month to month."

"How exciting."

"It is. However, there has been one snag."

"What?"

"Cal McCue," she said.

"What of him?" He met Cal at Alex and Matt's marriage, and remembered Matt's friend and colleague quite well.

"He had to be called away. Something to do with his family's ranch."

"How is Jack taking his absence?" It had been very apparent that Jack harbored feelings for Cal, but John knew of no courtship between the two.

Lou turned to him, a wry smile playing on her lips. "She's moping."

"I don't believe it. Moping is never a word I would use in reference to your sister."

"I wouldn't believe it true had I not seen it with my own eyes." She squinted out the window. "John?"

Hoping she was going to open up to him, he said, "Yes?" in his most consoling, comforting voice.

She looked oddly at him before pointing out the window. "Did I see earlier that you had papers in your pocket?"

His hands immediately sought his sermon, only to find it gone. Then he remembered that he had changed clothes, but could not recall having removed his sermon or the envelope that had arrived in yesterday's post.

He jumped to his feet.

"There are several papers stuck in the bush outside."

"My sermon!"

Lou's eyes widened, and she bolted out the back door before he could even think to stop her.

He followed quickly behind her, Dog at his heels.

Rain spit from the sky. The temperatures had dipped with the spring showers. It had gone from summer heat to the rawness of late fall in the course of an hour.

Lou picked a piece of damp paper from the bushes. "It seems to be melting," she called out as a blob of paper fell to the ground like an errant snowflake.

John swiped the rain from his eyes as he scanned the landscape. "Look for an envelope!" His sermon he knew by heart, but that envelope . . . He peeked under a holly bush, getting pricked for his troubles. He didn't stop to think why he cared so much about that envelope. Its contents wouldn't change his decision, but his grandmother's letters were his only communication from home, and he cherished them.

In the time since he bought the house, the grounds hadn't become overrun despite his neglect of them. One of the Parkers had lovingly tended a small patch of land beneath the kitchen window. This is where he found the fourth page of his sermon and watched it disintegrate between his fingers as the clouds above continued their onslaught.

"I found it!" Lou cried.

John searched for her, but couldn't immediately locate her. "Lou?"

"Up here," she called, her voice strong, musical.

Perched atop a low branch, she sat, holding aloft a white envelope.

His heart quite surely stopped. One false move on her part and she would tumble down. The fall was bound to break something.

Rain molded her hair to her face, his shirt to her skin as she sat, beaming at her find. "Is this what you were looking for?"

"Yes," he choked out. "Please come down from there, Lou." He spoke softly as to not frighten her in any way and cause her to lose her balance.

Rain drizzled down his face as he watched Lou scoot across the branch.

"Slowly," he cautioned. He positioned himself beneath her. If she were to tumble, he would break her fall.

His letter, which seemed so unimportant now that Lou was in danger, was held tightly between her teeth.

Staring up, it took him a moment to realize that she had stopped moving.

Her wide gaze looked down at him, a trace of fear evident amongst the obvious humor. Her violet eyes fairly twinkled in the dim light.

"Lou?"

A smile played on her lips. Her slim shoulders arched in a shrug. "Mmnm shhtuck."

He stared blankly at her, trying to decipher her words as they vibrated through the sodden envelope.

She waffled on the branch, causing his heart to cease all beats. His breath hitched.

After plucking the letter from her mouth, she tucked it into her voluminous shirt and said, quite clearly, "I'm stuck."

His fear fled as she shrugged helplessly, giving him one of those smiles he loved.

He remembered quite suddenly why she *was* here. *For I have a favor of the utmost importance to ask of you.*

He'd have to ask her about that when she was finally settled on firm ground.

"I'll come up," he offered.

"No." She jerked slightly to the left, then to the right.

Apprehension had the muscle in his jaw pulsing. "I'm coming up." He stepped toward the wide trunk of the tree.

"No, just give me a second . . ." She reached behind her. Dog began to growl low in his throat. John hushed him.

"Just one more . . ." She wiped the rain from her eyes. "The fabric is snagged on a branch."

Dog's growls increased in intensity. Thunder drummed the air from a distance. John moved beneath Lou, arms outstretched.

Dog pranced in a nervous circle.

"Down," John ordered him. He was nervous enough about Lou without having to worry about the dog too.

Lou tugged on the waistband of the pants. John heard a loud rip and Lou's muffled scream.

John automatically braced himself for her weight as he

watched her tumble off the branch, only to be surprised when she didn't land on him.

Dog began to bark furiously now as John looked up and saw Lou dangling upside-down, frantically trying to keep her shirt from slipping above her head.

The envelope she had tucked away swayed feather-like to the ground.

Despite her predicament, she wore a big, beautiful smile. "This could be fun . . . in other circumstances. I used to love climbing this tree when I was younger."

He couldn't believe she was calmly conversing as though she weren't strung upside down like a Christmas goose. He reached up for her just as her eyes went round as half dollars. It took a moment for him to realize she was slipping right out of her pants.

He caught her as she dropped and they both toppled to the ground like a felled tree. Wet grass soaked through the back of his shirt, his pants, but he paid it no heed, for he had her in his arms. A predicament, he found, he rather enjoyed.

Above his head, Lou's pants—rather, *his* pants—dangled comically from the tree limb.

Crimson stained Lou's cheeks. Timidly, she said, "Nice catch." She sat up, still with a leg on each side of him, as Dog's growling turned to a frightened whine. "Dog?"

Rain glistened off her bare legs. Pieces of grass clung to her smooth skin.

"Dog?" she called again, and John looked to where Dog was hunkered next to them, crouched low to the ground, his teeth bared.

Lou shifted on top of John, and he tried valiantly to ignore the shamefully pleasing effects her movements produced.

"What is it, boy?" he asked.

Dog seemed to be looking at something near the house.

Lou turned, her eyes widening. Her breath caught.

John turned just in time to see a man emerge from the shadows of the house, his hat pulled low, but not low enough to cover the censure in his eyes or the obvious resentment at what he witnessed.

Even as she sat atop him, Lou smiled and her chin lifted. "Why, hello."

The man stopped beside them and bent down. He grabbed the letter from the wet earth and wiped it on his pants, leaving a smear of mud and several blades of grass stuck to his trousers.

John looked up into the dark, hollow eyes he'd hoped to never see again.

"I believe this is yours, Reverend," Hank Burnett said.

Chapter Five

"Shall I take off my clothes now?"

Lou gaped at the woman. "Pardon?"

Dressed in a lavender gown, cut shockingly low at the throat, Daphne Caudill began to slide her stockings from her legs.

"Stop that!" Lou cried, looking around the room though she knew they were but the only occupants. If anyone were to witness this display, she'd be mortified. Especially with the gossip in River Glen having already decided that Lou's choice of a singer would also double as a harlot.

Confusion swept across Daphne's youthful features. "But I thought—"

Lou tried to sound prim. "This is not that sort of establishment, Miss Caudill. The singer we choose will be of the highest caliber, talent, and reputation."

Though that had been Lou's goal, finding a woman to fill the job had been difficult thus far. She'd interviewed well over a dozen women and found each one lacking in some regard.

She nibbled her lip. A lock of blond hair fell into her

line of sight as she stared at her list of interviewees. Absently she brushed the lock aside.

"I apologize," Daphne muttered.

Lou realized the young woman was blushing with embarrassment. "Please do not," she allowed. "You didn't know."

"Back in Chicago, it is policy to remove one's clothing when performing for gentlemen."

A sudden tide of anger swamped Lou with emotion. "That is appalling."

A tear trickled down Daphne's cheek. She nodded. "I had been hoping to gain other employment." Her voice was earnest. "I know I am not the best singer, but I was hoping I could ride this steamboat to another port and find work."

Lou rubbed her temples. Silently, she admitted that she had been nothing but coldly professional during the interviews. Her mood was foul, her temper already sparked by the debacle at John Hewitt's house the day before. Not to mention the scene that took place when she arrived back at the steamboat.

How could her sisters send Hank Burnett after her like she was some sort of animal who needed a short leash? It was insulting. Embarrassing.

Inwardly, she groaned.

"I should go," Daphne said.

"Wait." Lou rose from her chair. "I cannot offer you the job for which you interviewed; however, if you are serious about looking for another source of employment, perhaps I can help."

"How so?"

Lou paced. "How are you with food?"

Smiling, Daphne said, "I work well with food. It doesn't pinch."

Lou laughed, liking the woman immediately. She guessed them to be similar in age, though Daphne had an air of maturity about her Lou never dreamed she herself could possess.

"We are looking for both cooks and servers for the main dining room. I can all but guarantee that the food shall not pinch, unless," she smiled, "we are serving lobster or crab. However, I cannot guarantee that our passengers will keep their hands to themselves. I would like to think that the men aboard will be gentlemen, but as I'm sure you're well aware, there can be lechers lurking beneath the most polished façades."

"Oh yes, Miss Parker, I am well aware of that fact." Daphne smiled brightly. "I would be honored to work for you, for your family. When do I begin?"

Though the *Amazing Grace* was not due for its inaugural journey for another three weeks, Lou knew she could not turn this woman out. "Be here first thing in the morning. I will show you around. You can work with Doc in the kitchen, learning recipes and such. And please, call me Lou."

Lou escorted her to the door. She would not insult the woman by suggesting she wear something more appropriate for the kitchens. If Daphne did not already know, she would learn soon enough.

"You're so kind. Thank you," Daphne said, walking out the door, her gaze lowered.

Lou bit back a sigh, wishing she could simply bestow confidence upon the woman, but knew Daphne would have to achieve it herself.

"So you've finally found someone?"

Lou turned, a groan on her lips as her older sister Alex swept into the room like a miniature tornado. "No, I haven't."

Lou took a seat at the table. She pretended to look at the list of singers, but inwardly she was hoping Alex would just go away.

"You're still upset." Alex sat down and folded her hands on the table.

Glancing up, Lou noticed that Alex fairly glowed with joy. It had been a month since she married Matt Kinkade and her happiness shone in her brown eyes.

Before marrying Matt, Lou had considered Alex a beautiful woman. At twenty-five, her older sister was wise beyond her years, a dreamer at heart, and too modest for her own good. Now, after the marriage, Alex was exquisite. Her whole demeanor had shifted from one hoping to find love to one who loved intensely . . . and was loved that way in return. Matt Kinkade was a lucky man.

And her sister was a lucky woman.

That, however, didn't change Lou's feelings at the moment. "Yes, I'm still upset."

She folded the corner of the writing paper, noting she had only one woman left to interview. Why was it proving to be such a difficult task?

"We were worried about you. There were tornado sightings."

"You never would have sent someone after Jack."

Alex met her gaze. "No, you're right," she said frankly. "I wouldn't have."

Lou hadn't expected Alex to agree, though she should have known better. Alex, above all else, was honest as the day she was born.

Lou jumped to her feet. She breathed deeply, reining in her temper before she lashed out, as she had yesterday in the reverend's bathroom.

Her hands went to her face as she felt the swift heating of her cheeks.

"I am a grown woman," Lou said, more to herself than her sister. She turned to Alex, who rose from her chair, looking serene, which goaded Lou's ire further.

"I am beginning to see that, Lou." Alex shook her head,

her long, dark brown hair sweeping across her back. "But you are still my sister."

Alex stepped closer. She had not only inherited their father's looks, but his height as well. Lou had to look up at her, and when she did, she was surprised to see moisture in her sister's eyes.

"I have been too wrapped up in my own life to see that I've been a terrible sister."

Lou's anger fled. "Nonsense."

"It is true. I've been blind to certain things."

Lou walked over to the stage where her songstress would perform, should she ever actually hire someone. She turned her back to her sister. "Such as?" she said softly.

"The fact that you're a mature woman, one capable of finding her way to and from home."

Lou turned to gauge Alex's sincerity.

Alex bent over and picked a piece of lint from her light blue pants. "I also think I've never really seen you for who you are."

"And who am I?" Lou had to wonder at Alex's reaction should she ever learn of her behavior the day before. What would Alex say when she finally recognized the feisty spitfire Lou had been secretly harboring?

Alex tipped her head, staring. "I'm not sure. But I've only just realized you're not the quiet mouse I thought you were. I've seen it ever since we took on the *Amazing Grace*. Your strength, your loyalty, and your need to see where you fit in. Am I right?"

She could easily lie, say she was in fact a shy wallflower, but she had longed for this conversation for years. "Yes."

"Then why have you been pretending, Lou?"

Lou ran her hand over the stage. The cool dark wood chilled her palms. She shrugged. "I really didn't know any other way to fit in. You were the wise, smart one. Jack was the headstrong adventurer, and me? I was a sickly child, close to Mama." She had been born too early, and had been ill for the first ten years of her life. It wasn't until then that her father had taken her under his tutelage, teaching her all the things her sisters had learned years before. The archery, baseball, and astronomy. She never did catch up entirely, much to his dismay.

"Early on, I was labeled the timid one, the beautiful little doll too fragile too touch. Mama knew me, my dreams, and encouraged me, but then she died, and no one knew."

Not entirely the truth, but it would do for now. "I need to set up for my next interview. If you don't mind," she said to her sister.

Alex smiled gently. "And there's yet another thing I never knew about you."

Intrigued, Lou asked, "What's that?"

"How easily you can maneuver your way out of a conversation."

Lou's smile faltered. "Alex?"

She stopped on her way to the door. "Yes?"

"Did—did Hank say anything to you . . . about yesterday?"

A dark eyebrow arched. "Should he have?"

Lou shook her head. "No."

"Good luck finding a singer," Alex called as she closed the door behind her.

Hank Burnett.

Simply saying the man's name in his head had John clenching his teeth. And the notion that he was a *friend* of Lou's? It was enough to turn any man's stomach.

John pushed away from his desk, rising in quiet fury. Dog lifted his head, looked about, and dropped his jaw onto his paws once again.

How had this come to be? John wondered. Couldn't the Parkers perceive the type of man Hank embodied? Couldn't they see through his bland expression to the evil that lurked beneath the surface?

Of course not.

How could they? Hank hid it so well. John would not know of Hank's deceptions either, except Hank had sought him out upon his arrival in River Glen to seek absolution. And the bonds that allowed John to hear the horrid things Hank said were also the ones that now rendered him silent.

The old wood floor beneath the thin carpeting creaked beneath his pacing boots. There had to be some way to alert Lou to the danger she was in. Some way to warn her to stay away from Hank Burnett.

At all costs.

A ripple of fear rolled down his spine. He would think of something, he had to.

John sat back down. What remained of his sermon lay on his desk in tiny lumps as he tried to reconstruct his homily. He dipped his pen into the inkwell and wrote two words before Lou's image in the tree came to him, blocking out all other thoughts.

Lou Parker was an intriguing enigma. A delicate fawn, a courageous lion. She amazed him on so many levels.

Pulling open a drawer, he removed what was left of his grandmother's letter—a snowball-looking mass that was not only unreadable, but also now starting to crumble as it dried.

Lou's foray up the tree had been for naught.

Not that he minded. Her fall into his arms had been worth the loss of his sermon and the letter.

A loud chime echoed through the empty house. Dog rattled to his feet, his ears drawn back.

"Stay," John said.

Dog whimpered as John closed the door to the study behind him. His movements echoed through cavernous hall as he made his way to the foyer.

He pulled open the door and schooled his face into one of welcome, when in actuality he wished to close the door on this most unwelcome guest.

"Hello, Mrs. Farrell," he said.

"Indeed." She brushed past him, making her way into the house, her skirts trailing a riverbed of mud on the floor. She marched straight into the parlor and about-faced.

"Why, there's not one stick of furniture to sit upon."

John tucked his hands into his pockets and rocked on his heels. "No."

She tipped her head so far to the right, John feared her elaborately feathered hat would soon be on the floor.

"Why ever not?"

He untucked one hand and gestured to his study. "I haven't the time to shop." He hoped the lie would pass muster. He wasn't accustomed to telling falsehoods, but he felt the need was justified in this particular case. Mrs. Farrell need not know of his money woes.

"Well, this is highly unusual, I daresay."

He nudged open the door to the study a bit wider to accommodate her girth. Dog pulled his ears back and growled.

"Shoo!" Mrs. Farrell poked at Dog with her cane. Dog leaped to his arthritic feet and darted from the room.

John bit back a sharp retort. "What brings you by today?"

She opened a rather large reticule and fished about inside. Finally, she pulled several envelopes from the depths and held them aloft. "These."

"What, may I ask, are those?" he asked, noting the red tingeing Mrs. Farrell's bulbous nose.

"These are the apples with which Eve tempted Adam."

John sat. He didn't think he could have this conversation standing up. "Pardon?"

She shoved them onto his desk and settled herself in the

only other chair in the room. John opened one of the envelopes and his heart lurched into his throat.

"I will not have her influencing our young. She contacted young Hex Goolens, a rather impressionable young man to say the least, and made him an accomplice to her crimes."

He cleared his throat. "They're simply tickets to a baseball game. Miss Parker has committed no crime whatsoever, and she meant no harm, Mrs. Farrell."

"That remains to be seen."

He drew in a deep breath and offered up a brief prayer asking for patience. "What is it that you hold against her?"

She huffed. "Her mere presence is an insult to me."

He found that to be an odd comment, but probed no deeper.

"The tickets must be returned at once, and Reverend, you must speak to her about never contacting the youth of this community again."

"I'm afraid I can't do that, Mrs. Farrell."

Her eyes bulged, apparently at the lack of his compliance. "You most certainly will, or I will speak to the church council."

He rose. "Then do so." He spoke the words softly, but they held weight and conviction that even a deaf man could hear.

Mrs. Farrell's scowl suddenly disappeared into one of her many chins. A smile crept across her face. "This is all part of your plan, isn't it, Reverend?"

Plan? He had no idea what she was speaking about. Then he remembered.

I was hoping you would speak to them, perhaps. Show them the error of their ways, perhaps befriend *them as part of a master plan to finally be rid of them once and for all.*

Did she really think he'd thought of a plan to rid the community of the Parkers? For the first time, he questioned not only her judgment, but also her sanity.

However, this 'plan' might be in his, not to mention the Parkers', best interest. Mrs. Farrell would never know that his agenda vastly differed from her own.

He cleared his throat in preparation for his second lie of the day. "Yes, Mrs. Farrell, it is all part of *my* plan."

Lou looked at her watch fob pinned to her blouse. Time was ticking away and she still needed to find Hank. She had but one interview remaining, then she would to seek him out. With hope, it wouldn't be too late. She'd hate to have to wait until Monday to speak to him about what he had seen at John's house.

And convince him not to say anything to anyone that would jeopardize the reverend's reputation.

The ride back to the *Amazing Grace* had been a silent one, the air filled with crackling tension. Lou had been hurt by her sisters' interference, and she had been angry at Hank's interruption. For a moment there on that cold wet grass, she had been sure John was going to kiss her.

Would he have?

Would she have let him?

Oh, she knew the answer to that question, though she tried telling herself she would have pushed him away, as was proper.

She hopped up on the stage and looked out into the empty room. Burgundy curtains stood sentry beside her. Empty tables and chairs waited for the use of patrons.

Standing like this, she felt free. There were no expectant faces peering at her, no voices whispering.

A lyric came to mind and she allowed herself to sing it aloud. The sound echoed across the room, and Lou listened as the note resonated.

She had no audience. Furtively, she looked around. No one would know.

From deep in her soul, she released her song. As she

sang about love and loss, tears welled, as they always did when she allowed herself these rare moments of peace.

A knock interrupted her, and panic seized her throat. She darted behind the drapery, hoping no one had heard her.

"Lou?"

It was Jack. Lou's heart beat furiously as she wiped her eyes.

"Lou? Where are you?"

Jack's voice came nearer. She wasn't going to leave without looking behind the curtains. There was only one thing Lou could do. She shuffled her feet and called, "I'm coming."

A second later she appeared on the stage, looking down at her sister.

Jack lifted a dark eyebrow and peered into the corners of the stage. "Who was singing?"

Flustered, Lou said, "One of my interviewees." It was no surprise Jack hadn't recognized her voice. The only times her sisters heard her sing was en masse at church. Sweet, lilting hymns, nothing like the low sultry ballad she had just poured out. Apples and oranges entirely.

"Where is she?"

Lou swallowed, thinking fast. "She went out the back-stage door," she lied.

"What's her name?" Jack probed.

A name. Bertha? No. Caroline? Too plain. Sarah? No, no, no. She needed a name. Quickly.

"Lou? She does have a name, does she not?"

Lou wrung her hands. Her mother's voice whispered in her ear.

You've the voice of an angel.

"Angelique. Her name is Angelique."

"No last name?"

She tipped her chin. "Not that she told me."

Jack turned around, heading for the door. "Interesting. Hire her. She's wonderful."

A dark depression filled Lou. "I don't think she's going to workout."

"Why not?"

Why? Lou searched the recesses of her mind. Why? "She's ugly," she spat out. Then gasped that she had actually said such a thing aloud.

Jack's eyes widened in shock. "What did you just say?"

Trying not to back down in the face of her rudeness, Lou placed her hands on her hips. "I said she's ugly. Uglier than ugly. Hideous. She'd scare the passengers. The children would have nightmares."

Jack gave her a look. A look that easily screamed *What are you up to?* Instead of caving in as Lou had hoped, Jack said, "Be that as it may. Her voice is amazing. Put her in costume and slap a mask on her." She put her hands on her hips. "The men will be highly intrigued by her mysteriousness. Hire her, Lou."

A mask. A costume. No one would see her face, know her identity. A dizzying sense of excitement weakened her knees. She sat, her feet dangling over the edge of the stage.

"Oh," Jack said. "I had nearly forgotten why I came in here."

She could sing. Not only sing, but also perform. Until this point it had been merely a dream. As Angelique, Lou's dreams could become real.

"You have a visitor."

The words barely registered in Lou's mind. What would she wear? How could she disguise herself? A wig. Definitely, she needed a wig. And a mask. Energy swirled through her veins. Feathers. A mask with feathers.

"Lou!"

Her head jerked up at Jack's commanding tone. Lou gasped and jumped to the ground as she spotted John Hewitt smiling at her.

"As I said," Jack explained, "you have a visitor."

Chapter Six

"Reverend?" Lou's sweet voice held a note of question, though her eyes smiled at him.

Jack winked as she backed out of the room. The door closed behind him with a welcome click.

He looked around. "What a place you have here."

He followed her gaze as it swept about the room, wondering if she was looking at it through his eyes. The dark paneled walls, the thick carpeting, the bar lining the wall in the rear, empty now of its glasses and bottles. Most certainly a masculine room, but not entirely. The wrought iron wall sconces were of a floral nature, with generous curves and bowing. If one looked closely, the carpeting also boasted tiny florets every few yards. It was an intriguing mix, to be sure.

"Do you like it?" She turned her morning-glory eyes his way.

Staring back, lost in her amazing gaze, he said, "Very much."

They stood there in silence a bit longer before color swept up her neck, over her cheeks, and settled, finally, in the tips of her elflike ears.

"I'm sorry." The words escaped her lips in a rush. "Would you care to sit?"

Amazed, he watched as she actually pulled out a chair for him. When he hesitated, she apparently sensed her breach of etiquette. Her chin shot into the air and she practically flung herself into the nearest chair.

She tugged at the collar of her shirt, a green blouse with puffed sleeves and narrow wrists. Suddenly her movements stilled. "Why are you here, John?" she asked softly.

He'd asked himself that very question at least one hundred times on the ride here from River Glen. Was this something that couldn't be put off until tomorrow after church services? That was, if she attended services after what had transpired yesterday afternoon.

He pulled in a deep breath. "I'm here to return these." He slid the envelopes Mrs. Farrell had given him across the table.

Violet eyes widened as she peered inside, and his stomach ached as though a foot had just delivered a blow to his midsection.

"But these were for the boys. . . ." she said, her whisper carrying across the room, bouncing off the panels, wounding him again and again.

One by one, she pulled out the Cincinnati Reds tickets she had sent to the boys after yesterday's baseball game. She'd not only taught those boys a lesson on judging others, but by sending them the tickets even after she'd won the bet, she taught them a lesson on humility. One that had been completely destroyed by Mrs. Farrell and the others who thought ill of the Parkers for no apparent reason.

"I'm sorry," he said.

Her delicate hand crumpled one of the tickets. "It was Mrs. Farrell who returned these, wasn't it?"

Longing to reach across the table and take her hand, to take her hurt onto his own shoulders, he willed himself to remain still. "To be fair, it wasn't just Mrs. Farrell. Some of the parents were highly suspicious of your gift."

Lou shook her head. "I will never understand."

He feared he was coming to the same conclusion.

She closed her eyes and covered her cheeks with her hands. "Why else are you here, John?"

"The tickets . . ."

Her eyes fluttered open and he could see the pain in their depths. What would she say if he pulled her into his arms, comforted her? Would she turn away? Or return his embrace? "You could have given them to me tomorrow after services."

He couldn't argue. Though he had tried telling himself that she might not show up at church, she had too strong a spirit to allow an embarrassing situation to temper her actions.

The truth of the matter had always been there, under the surface, simply waiting to be revealed. He had wanted to come here, to her, to see for himself just exactly how good of a friend Hank Burnett was to Lou.

However, he couldn't simply come out and say so, now could he? He needed an excuse for his presence, and quickly. "Yesterday," he began.

She laughed, startling him. "Yesterday was . . ."

A disaster? An embarrassment? A rather large mistake?

"Amazing," she said on a sigh.

"Amazing?" It was not in the least what he expected her to say.

"The most fun I've had in ages." She propped her elbows on the table, green fabric flouncing. "That is, if you exclude how it ended."

With her in his arms and Hank Burnett standing over them. He wondered which she considered the exclusion. Being in his arms or Hank's presence?

His conscience nagged him. He would have kissed her

if Hank hadn't appeared. Under the beech tree, in the rain, thunder rolling across the hills, he would have kissed her.

Briefly, he closed his eyes—not in penance, as he should be doing, but in remembrance of the feel of her skin, the echo of her laughter.

He opened his eyes to find her staring at him, her light lashes lowered ever so slightly. Her gaze warm, intoxicating.

Just then the door banged open. Guilt had John jumping to his feet. Lou sat, the light in her eyes suddenly replaced with blatant aggravation.

"Hello, Reverend," Matt Kinkade said, strolling into the room, shaking his hand vigorously. "I didn't know we had a visitor." He looked to Lou.

She slowly rose to her feet. "Liar, liar."

John's neck snapped as he jerked his head back and forth between the two.

Matt pushed a large hand through his hair. He smiled—a slight rising of the upper corners of his lips—at Lou. "I told Alex it was a bad idea, but she insisted I come in and find out why Reverend Hewitt is here." He looked expectantly at John.

Before he could say anything, Lou said, "I was just trying to find out the same thing."

In identical gestures, both Matt and Lou turned to face him, arms folded across their chests.

"I, uh—" He spoke rapidly, the words tumbling out. "Lou had mentioned yesterday at the baseball game that she needed to ask a favor."

He adopted Matt's stance and turned in tandem with the *Amazing Grace*'s captain to look at Lou.

"Really now," Matt said. "Baseball and favors? Have you been keeping secrets, Lou?"

* * *

"Secrets?" Lou managed a slight laugh. Her heart pounded. If they only knew what she had planned. She turned on her heel and headed for the stage, pushing in chairs as she walked past. "Hardly, gentlemen."

"Did she pitch?" Matt asked John.

John nodded. "Quite well."

"You should see Jack hit." Matt shook his head.

"And Alex?" John asked. "What does she do?"

From halfway across the room, Lou saw a smile creep into Matt's eyes, a smile that came from deep within his soul. "Alex," Matt said, "doesn't have any *one* strength. She does it all well."

Lou watched in fascination as the men conversed. They seemed to have forgotten that she still remained in the room.

John scratched his chin. "Is your family coming to the church picnic in two weeks' time, Captain? I'd love to round up a baseball game."

Lou's shoulders stiffened. Matt's gray gaze slid to her. "I'm not sure," he said, "if that's a good idea, Reverend."

"Why not?" John looked at Lou, saw her stiff stance, yet continued on undeterred. "I think it's just what River Glen needs." His voice dropped. "Just what the Parkers need."

Matt hedged. "I'll have to talk it over with Alex. Not to mention Jack." He grinned. "I can already see by Lou's expression what her opinion is on the matter." He stretched out his hand. John shook it as Matt said, "I'll leave you be now."

Lou finally spoke. "And what will you tell Alex about the reverend's visit?" she asked her brother-in-law. She could only imagine what her sisters would have to say about this visit. Jack had already surmised Lou's feelings for John. Could Alex see through her too?

Matt winked. "You'll see."

Lou groaned as he closed the door behind him. She felt

John's warm gaze on her and looked up to find him staring. His deep blue eyes caused her heart to thrum, her pulse to beat wildly.

She had wondered if she'd still react to him as she had done yesterday. Her body seemed to come alive when he was near, and she wasn't all that sure what to make of it.

"I take it," he said, "that baseball was one of your father's many lessons?"

His voice washed over her as it echoed about the room. How was it that they seemed to end up alone so often? "He adored the game."

"He taught you well."

"Thank you. I didn't have nearly as many lessons as my sisters, as I was a sickly child, but baseball I mastered."

He walked slowly toward the stage. "It shows."

Her palms dampened with his every step. A whirlwind of emotion blew about her chest, rising, rising, longing to be released.

It confused yet excited her at the same time. It was a new sensation, one she longed to release and explore. Her gaze landed on John's lips. What would they feel like upon her own? How would he taste?

As she realized the direction of her thoughts, a fierce heat swept up her throat and covered her cheeks.

His arm brushed her sleeve. "You look lovely today, Lou."

She looked down at what she wore. A green blouse and loose, cream-colored pants that flared over her leather boots. The clothes were years old, but she never had to worry about the dictates of fashion, as she and her sisters had never followed conventional etiquette in that area.

"Thank you," she said.

The lines on his forehead crinkled as he said, his expression quite serious, "Have you always worn slacks?"

Though she assumed he'd heard all the gossip surrounding her family, his question sounded sincere. "Since I could walk," she said. "All of us. Father thought it absurd to dress us as miniature dolls, only to have our clothing ruined when we hiked or camped or went riding."

He turned toward her, his arm once again brushing against her. The touch sent an arrow of warmth straight to her heart. "Did you enjoy hiking and camping and riding?"

Truth be told, she never had much of a chance to do any of those things. She had been sick too often to do much other than stay in bed and read. She drew in a deep breath. "I really don't know all that much about you, John," she said, hoping to change the subject to one that interested her much more. "Where are you from?"

It was if he had slipped on a mask. Gone was the sincerity and caring, replaced now with a closed-off look, disinterested and bland. She recognized the concealment of emotions when she saw it and had to wonder what he was hiding from her.

"John?"

He blinked. "New York. I'm from New York."

"What part?"

"Southern."

"The city?" she queried, intrigued by this change in him. "Is that where your parents live?"

"My mother died when I was seven. My grandmother, my mother's mother, moved in and helped my father raise me. They are all the family I have, and yes, that's where they live." He cleared his throat. "It's getting late, Lou. I—" He stared at her, his eyebrows dipping. He hooked a thumb over his shoulder. "I really ought to be going."

Her chest tightened. What had she said to make him run away? "Okay," she said softly.

He swallowed, his Adam's apple bobbing. He nodded and spun around. His strides were sure and quick as he crossed the room, a man escaping.

Abruptly, he stopped. Lou took a step toward him but held herself back. She suddenly realized the power John had over her and it frightened her. For he had the power to break her heart, and she didn't think she could survive it twice, the first being at the hand of her father.

"Lou?" His fists clenched. It was as if he warred within himself and determination had won over retreat.

Moisture pooled in her eyes, and she hoped he couldn't see it. "Yes?"

He cleared his throat. "You said you had a favor to ask of me? Yesterday, at the schoolhouse . . ."

"Yes, I do."

"Are you hungry?"

She laughed at the sudden change of subject. "Yes." She swiped at her eyes, wiping away the wetness.

"There a small restaur—"

"What's wrong?" she asked when he broke off.

Crimson caressed his cheeks.

"What is it, John?"

"It's quite embarrassing, that's what it is. I've not brought enough money with me to dine out. I'm afraid it will have to be another time."

His honesty wooed her like nothing else. "Nonsense. We'll eat in the galley." She tipped her head. "I can fix you something."

Finding Hank would have to wait, she reflected, and her next interview wasn't scheduled for another hour. She had the time, and she was more than willing to spend it with John Hewitt.

He smiled. "There's nothing I would like more."

She stretched out her hand, her heart turning over again and again as he slipped his hand into it, loving his warmth, his strength. "Then let's go," she said.

Chapter Seven

Nearly a week later, Lou found Daphne in the kitchen beating a filet of chicken breast with a rubber mallet.

"Daphne?"

The young beauty looked up, her fiery red hair tumbling into her face. "Miss Parker! What brings you down here? Not fixing to make lunch, I hope."

Lou cringed. "Please call me Lou, and no, I'm not going to prepare another lunch." Obviously word had spread in the week since Lou had made lunch for herself and John about her complete lack of culinary skills.

How was she to know that the meat Doc had left on the galley counter had been set aside as fish bait because it had spoiled? Luckily for her, she rarely ate meat and had eaten only fruit and vegetables that day.

But poor John . . .

"Has the reverend recovered?"

Lou walked over to the dumbwaiter and tugged on the handle. Oh, how she wished she could ride up to the dining hall once again, but she reined in the urge. If she wanted John to see her as respectable, she needed to start behaving that way.

67

"Lou?"

Lost in her thoughts, she started at Daphne's voice. "Oh, I'm sorry. The reverend?" She gnawed her lip. "I'm not sure how he's faring. I've not seen him since . . ." She shrugged. "Well, you know."

She had received a letter from him, asking her to take over his baseball games for the week, but she had not laid eyes on him since she nearly killed him with her cooking.

Tapping her finger on the countertop, she said, "I'm sure he is well enough for services tomorrow." At least she hoped so.

Daphne laid down her mallet and washed the chicken from her hands. "I'm sure he will."

"Will you be joining us?"

Wide ice-blue eyes blinked. "Me?"

Lou laughed. "Of course."

"Will I be welcome? My background . . ."

Sighing, Lou said, "In River Glen, one is never truly welcomed. But in the church, you always are. Your past is just that, Daphne: in the past. Let it be and move on with your life."

A smile bloomed on Daphne's face. "Thanks to you and your family, I can."

"You took the first step."

Daphne looked down, her red hair falling down her shoulders. "You're right."

Slowly Daphne's confidence was building, but Lou suspected it would take much more than a steady, honest job to complete the undertaking.

"Actually," Lou said brightly, "that's why I'm here."

"It is?"

"I need your help."

Nervous excitement had kept her awake many a night in the last week as she stealthily gathered all the things she needed to transform into Angelique. Madame Angelique,

Lou amended silently. She had added the 'Madame' to give herself a bit more mystery. It seemed to be working. Buzz aboard the steamboat was high about Madame Angelique. And buzz meant business. Word would spread, customers would fill the steamboat.

Yet, when she tried Madame Angelique's costume on, she looked an utter fool. She needed help. Help from someone who knew the world of lounges, and could help Lou turn into a sultry songstress.

"With what?" Daphne asked.

"With me." It would be a risk, taking Daphne into her confidence, but it was one Lou was willing to take.

"Let's put on a kettle, and I'll tell you all about it."

Over a cup of tea, Lou explained her plans, her dreams. Daphne's excitement to help only caused the nervous butterflies in Lou's stomach to beat their wings harder.

She drew in a deep breath. "So you'll help?"

"I'd love to. I have many id—"

Daphne broke off, her eyes narrowing, her body seeming to shrink inside itself. "Daphne? Are you all right?" She looked ill, and Lou's first thought was that she had poisoned her too, until she realized that Daphne had been the one to make the tea.

A male voice said, "Lou."

Lou jumped in fright as the voice came from directly behind her; she'd not heard anyone enter the room. She spun and came face to face with the opaque eyes of a dead trout. Several dead trout.

Though her legs were a bit shaky, she stood. Hank thrust the string of fish toward her.

"I caught them for you."

Reluctantly, Lou reached out a hand. "Uh, er, thank you."

"I'll take those for you." Daphne snatched the fish from her, and before Lou could make proper introductions,

Daphne disappeared around a corner of the galley, heading toward the iceboxes.

Hank rocked on his heels, and Lou swallowed a lump of guilt. She had been avoiding him. Although she told herself she would seek him out, plead for his silence, she had stayed clear of him instead. As far as she knew, he'd held his tongue about what he'd seen, and she was beyond grateful.

"Thank you for the fish. I'm sure they'll be wonderful." Not that she'd eat any of it, since she'd given up eating meat years before.

He rocked on his heels. "I have a fishing cabin with a trout pond. Maybe you'd like to see it someday?"

She pushed aside the refusal perched on the tip of her tongue. She nodded. "Perhaps when we return from St. Louis?"

He smiled, the first she'd ever seen. Small white teeth gleamed. "All right then." He tipped his hat. "Good day."

No sooner had he left did Daphne appear at her elbow. "Watch out for that one, Lou. He's trouble."

Lou stared at the door Hank had just exited. "Do you really think so?"

Daphne wore a look that revealed all she had witnessed in her young life. "I know so."

Later the following week, Lou shifted in her pew, well aware of the spiteful gazes boring into the back of her head. She could just kick Alex for wanting to arrive at church early to speak to John about the picnic after the service. And she could strangle Jack with her bare hands for claiming a seat in the front pew. Normally they sat in the rear of the church, away from prying eyes.

She tried to pretend the stares didn't bother her as she watched John read a passage from the Old Testament. Guilt gnawed at her conscience. It had been two weeks since she had seen him, and he still looked a bit pale.

His voice boomed over the congregation as he closed the Bible and launched into a sermon about forgiveness and acceptance. She gathered the forgiveness portion was aimed at her family, the acceptance at the townsfolk.

By the scowls on the faces surrounding her, John's message wasn't getting through.

The picnic was going to be a nightmare.

Forget kicking Alex. She wanted to stuff her in the nearest steamer trunk and toss the key into the Ohio. What had Alex been thinking by agreeing to come to the picnic in the first place? And to play a ball game versus the townspeople? Was she insane?

Lou stole a glance at Alex. Matt held her sister's hand tightly, and a stab of envy swept through Lou as she watched her brother-in-law's thumb trace tiny circles on her sister's palm.

She sighed.

Jack leaned in. "Stop fidgeting."

Lou frowned. "I can't believe we're here doing this," she whispered. She should have stayed with Daphne aboard the *Amazing Grace*. Daphne had had the foresight to plead a headache and stayed in bed, though Lou felt her absence had more to do with not wanting to socialize and little to do with head pain.

"Shhh!" Jack chastised. "You're being rude."

Guiltily, Lou looked up to see John looking her way. He continued talking, but she saw a definite hint of a smile. She smiled back and silently vowed to be on her best behavior. She didn't want to embarrass him. On the contrary, she wanted to set a good example.

If only she knew how.

She was a fool if she didn't admit she had feelings for John. She most surely did. It was in her best interest to gain, if not friendship, then acceptance of the people in this very room. For if she didn't, she and John would never have a future.

Absently, she realized people were rising to their feet. Jack tugged on her arm and opened her hymnal to share with her. Lou timidly sang the hymn, never allowing her voice its full range. To do so would call attention, and that was the very last thing she wanted.

The service ended and Lou watched John walk down the center aisle and pause at the set of white paneled doors to offer greetings to those who had attended as they exited.

Having sat in the front pew, Lou was one of the last ones out behind Jack, Alex, and Matt.

He took her hand as she approached and gave it a warm squeeze. "Good morning, Miss Parker."

"Hello." She gazed up at him hopefully. "Are you feeling much better?"

He graced her with a wide smile and his blue gaze warmed her to the tips of her toes. "I am. Cora took great care of me. Thank you for recommending her."

Cora had been the Parker family housekeeper since Lou slept in a cradle. It had nearly broken Lou's heart to release the older woman from employment when they received word of their father's bankruptcy. "Thank you for taking her in. I hated to ask it of you, but I felt so badly for her, and guilty that we had to dismiss her in the first place." Ask? She had practically forced John to take Cora on, over-stepping the bounds of friendship, yet he hadn't minded.

He took her elbow and guided her down the steps where people had gathered in tiny clumps, conversing. No doubt about her and her family, Lou thought, disheartened.

"Cora knows full well that you simply didn't have the funds to keep her on, and she also explained to me that you offered her a position aboard the *Amazing Grace* once you returned from New Orleans with the decision to turn the boat into a floating hotel."

Lou colored at the admiration she heard in his voice. She didn't deserve it—she had done what any person would do when they cared greatly for another. "She must have also told you how she turned me down?"

He nodded.

She scuffed at the ground, sending small plumes of dust into the air that settled on the cuffs of her blue trousers. "Not that I blame her in the least. Her whole family is here. Her sons, her grandchildren. She didn't want to leave them. But then I thought of you, and hadn't heard that you hired help. . . ."

He squinted against the bright May sun. "You needn't explain, Lou," he said softly.

"Okay." She smiled.

John eyed the basket she carried on her elbow. "Dare I ask?"

She sighed. "This is all Alex's idea."

"The picnic basket auction?"

Glumly, she nodded.

He covered his mouth with his left hand, trying quite abysmally to cover the smile lurking beneath his fingers. "Dare I ask how she blackmailed you into going along with this idea?"

Lou started. "How did you know?"

He didn't bother hiding his laugh. "It's the only way you would agree to such a thing."

She smiled despite herself. "She threatened to take away the funding for the Gentlemen's Lounge if I didn't attend today." Oh, and she needed that money. She still had many things to purchase, from glassware to costumes.

His humor vanished. "She wouldn't really do such a thing, would she? Knowing how much the effort and care you've put in on that project?"

The conversation Lou had with Alex that morning came rushing back. Alex had been so adamant they try to fit in and get along with the people of River Glen that Lou had taken her threat seriously. "I'm not sure, but I didn't want to take the risk. I can suffer the humiliation of one afternoon."

For her dream of singing in front of a crowd, she would succumb to her sister's demand. Another week. That was all they had until the boat backed out of port for its maiden voyage as a hotel.

"Surely someone will bid on the basket."

John's voice snapped her out of her thoughts. "You think?"

She saw him swallow as he hedged about answering. "Surely *someone* will."

She wanted to laugh. He apparently thought she had made the lunch within the basket, as was custom. Well, she hadn't planned on making that mistake twice and had asked Daphne to put something together. Something that wouldn't poison the purchaser.

"If solely for the pleasure of your company, someone will bid," he said. A tickle of suspicion swept down Lou's spine. She shivered in the afternoon heat. "Pardon? Pleasure of my company?"

John tucked his hands into the pockets of his black pants. The lines on his forehead crinkled together as he frowned. "Yes. Whoever bids highest on the basket gets to eat lunch with the person who brought the basket. Didn't you know?"

"I've never been to a church picnic before," she said weakly.

Turning sharply on her heel, she searched the church grounds for Alex. She was easy to spot, being that she was so tall, and was looking her way. As Lou glared at her older sister, vowing a hundred ways of revenge, Alex looked quickly away, hunched over, and sidled into the crowd.

"She meant no harm."

Lou turned back to John. "That's a load of—"

His eyebrows arched.

She smiled sweetly. "Malarkey?"

He laughed. His dark hair shone in the sunlight, turning a honeyed brown. He'd added a coat to his usual clerical ensemble, and with his stiff stance, he looked older than his twenty-four years.

A shrill voice rose above the crowd. "Oh Reverend! Reverend!"

Lou braced herself as Mrs. Karpinsky came barreling through the crowd, towing a very lovely young woman behind her like she was a toy on a string.

"Reverend." Mrs. Karpinsky placed a hand on her heaving bosom as she trembled to a stop, the girl behind her stopping so short she nearly pitched over.

"Good day, Mrs. Karpinsky."

The older woman shot Lou a disparaging look. "So sorry for the interruption."

Lou deemed by the look of glee on the woman's face that she wasn't sorry at all. And as soon as Mrs. Karpinsky opened her mouth she knew why.

"I'd love you to meet my daughter, Belle. She's fresh home from finishing school."

The young woman blushed to the color of a cooked lobster. "Mama!" she protested.

"Pleasure to meet you," John said, bowing slightly.

Lou looked between the two, a flare of white-hot jealousy nearly blinding her. She had to admit Belle was beautiful. Of medium height with lustrous red hair and a pair of sparkling green eyes, Belle was simply stunning.

"Isn't she perfect, Reverend?"

Lou watched his reaction closely. "Indeed."

Something twisted painfully in Lou's stomach.

John smiled. "She has clearly inherited her looks from her lovely mother."

Lou nearly choked, seeing as Mrs. Karpinsky closely resembled a frog Lou had once caught. Belle didn't look too pleased by the compliment either.

Mrs. Karpinsky's hand fluttered to her mouth. Apparently, she had been caught off-guard as well.

Lou was feeling all was once again well in the world until John said, "I'd be honored, Miss Karpinsky, if you will save me a waltz at the dance tonight."

Belle beamed. "You waltz, Reverend?"

"I learned as a young boy."

Clapping her hands in delight, Belle said, "How wonderful!"

Dance? Waltz? Lou's stomach tumbled right down to her knees. She could hit a bulls-eye with a bow and arrow. She could hit a golf ball farther than her father, and she could swing a sword as though she had been a pirate in a former life, but dance? She knew nothing about dancing.

She touched John's shoulder and felt that now familiar heat seep through her skin and into her bloodstream. He turned to her. "Your sermon was lovely," she sputtered. She struggled to find words. "Good-bye!"

She turned quickly. Behind her she could hear Mrs. Karpinsky's voice mutter something about rudeness and poor upbringing. Lou walked as fast as she dared without breaking into a full run toward the small gazebo in the rear of the meadow, where she could hide for the rest of the afternoon.

John had no intention on bidding upon any basket. Beyond not having extra funds to waste, his attentions on one particular basket would cause rumors to abound.

His gaze, as it had all afternoon, slipped over the heads of others to watch Lou. She looked perfectly miserable. She stood off to the side, away from her family. It seemed to him that she was slowly easing left, toward the trees. Escaping.

With a smile on his face, he called over to young Tommy Beasley. He bent down and whispered in his ear. The lad looked a bit on the anxious side, but didn't dare refuse him.

Tommy ran up to Alex Kinkade and tapped her on the leg. Alex smiled down at the boy, then crouched to his level. Tommy cupped Alex's ear with his tiny hand as he whispered John's message.

Alex jumped to her feet, looking toward the tree line. "Lou! Lou!"

John smiled as Lou froze. He hated to do it to her, but it was for the best. She needed to shed some of her shyness, and this might just be the way to do it.

John turned as a heavy hand landed on his shoulder. Levi Mason, the town barber, greeted him. "So that's the way of it, is it, Reverend?" He shook his head. "There's gonna be some mamas none too pleased with this."

John followed the old man's gaze and saw Lou in a heated debate with her sister.

"She's a beauty, that's for sure. Looks just like her mama, she does."

John stammered. "I—uh, don't know what you're talking about, Levi."

Levi guffawed. "Surely you do. I don't go blaming you for not sayin' so." He dug his toe into the grass. "It's not gonna be easy."

John swallowed. Easy? A relationship with Lou, even courting, would be near impossible thanks to Mrs. Farrell and her command over the town.

Thankfully, Marcy Granger tapped a hammer on a wooden table, calling all to attention, including Levi, which John took as an answer to a prayer. The man might be old, but he was sharp. It had taken only one look from John toward Lou for the old man to see right through to John's feelings for her.

He stole a quick look around. How many others here could tell—see—what he was feeling?

Marcy called for all the picnic baskets for the auction to be placed on the table. John noticed it had taken a hard shove from Jack Parker to get Lou moving. She did so at a quick pace, and then she was back hiding behind her family in the blink of an eye.

He was doing it again.

Watching her.

He tugged at his tightening collar and forced himself to look elsewhere. He focused on Marcy and her bidding of the baskets and pretended not to notice the hint of a smile on Levi's weathered face.

"I ain't sayin' it can't be done." Levi rocked on his heels.

John leaned against the rough bark of a large oak tree, fearing he was going to need its support. He feigned ignorance. "What can't?"

"This here basket," Marcy intoned, "was made by Lindy Sue Miller. Ten cents? Do I hear ten cents?"

Levi didn't take his eyes off the basket. "Courting the lovely LouEllen."

Through a sudden coughing fit, John said, "I really don't—"

"Ten cents!" a voice in the crowd called out.

"Fifteen!" another voice countered.

Levi thumped John on the back. "All's to do is turn around Leona Farrell's pigheaded, mulish, obstinate opinions and all'll be right as rain."

"Twenty cents!" the first voice called out.

Was that a blush creeping up Levi's neck? Surely he didn't—It just wasn't possible. Yet . . . "You'll be knowing Mrs. Farrell well?"

"Twenty-one cents!"

It was! The old man was blushing. Inwardly jumping for joy, because this meant a change of a very uncomfortable subject, John smiled.

Levi swiped a hand though his snow-white hair. "We go back some."

"Twenty-two!"

A group of girls tittered over the bidding on Lindy Sue's basket. John looked over their heads and saw Lindy Sue herself turn the color of a beet.

He turned his attention back to Levi. "Do you know why Mrs. Farrell has such a strong dislike of the Parkers?"

"Twenty-three cents!" the first voice, sounding slightly desperate, called out.

The old man peered at him through clear, keen eyes. "Don't like gossiping like yon womenfolk."

"Thirty!"

"Oh, certainly not." John thought quickly. Levi had his pride to consider. "It's background information, is all. I'd like to mend fences . . . if I can."

Levi sized him up from under white bushy eyebrows. "Between you, me, and this here tree, Hiram Parker was a fine form of a man. You ever meet him?"

"No."

Marcy's voice called out, "Any other bids?" She looked around. "Sold!"

A round of applause crackled though the meadow. Perfunctorily, John clapped, not really paying attention now that he was finally going to understand the cause of the hatred aimed at the Parkers.

"Tall, handsome as the devil hisself. Women fair swooned when he walked by and smiled at them." He shook his head, though a smile lingered on his lips. "My best friend, he was."

"I didn't know."

"Only the old-timers recall."

Vaguely he heard another basket being auctioned, but the sounds of the afternoon faded as he listed to Levi. "Did you two have a falling out?"

"Of sorts. He was going to marry the woman I loved. And I didn't take too kindly to it. Made a big ol' fool of myself, I did."

"Grace Parker?"

Levi's clear eyes clouded. "Nah."

Levi's gaze wandered across the field and John followed it as if a leash led him. It focused on the one person John never would have suspected. "Mrs. Farrell!" he said, shocked. He turned to Levi. "Mrs. Farrell?"

Levi's chin dipped.

"Hiram Parker was going to marry Mrs. Farrell?"

"It's true."

Hiram Parker, Mrs. Farrell, and Levi Mason. John blinked in pure astonishment. "What happened? They never did marry, did they?"

Levi kicked at the grass, uprooting a big chunk of sod. "Hiram done ran off and left her the day before the wedding. Fell plum in love with one of the wedding guests."

Marcy pounded on the table, startling John. "This next basket was made by . . . Oh. It's made by Miss Lou Parker."

A hush fell over the meadow. John's pulse thrummed in his throat. Surely someone would bid on the basket. *Please, someone bid.*

His gaze sought Lou's. She stared at the ground, her whole face bathed in crimson.

"Ten cents?"

John definitely heard pity in Marcy's tone. Yes, Lou heard it too. Her small nub of a chin shot into the air. Her violet eyes blazed with indignity.

Footsteps pounded in rhythm to John's heart. Several

youngsters ran up to Levi and tugged on his pants. "They be needing you at the sawing races."

"I'll be right along." Levi shooed the children away. He turned to John. "You need to be a-biddin'."

The stubborn set of Lou's jaw tore at him. Someone had to bid.

Marcy looked around at the crowd. "Uh, five cents?"

"I—I can't. People will think—"

Levi took a step away. "So let them think it."

John opened his mouth to form a protest, but none came out.

"If Hiram hadn't up and run away with Grace, he'd have lost out on love itself. I done think he didn't much care what people thought."

"Two cents?" Marcy called out, pitifully.

John's gaze darted between Marcy, Lou, and Levi before Levi's words sunk in. His mouth dropped open. "But—"

Levi walked backward. "That means you be a fool not to accept what the Good Lord has put before you."

Just as Levi's parting words registered, a male voice in the middle of the crowd called out a bid. "Twenty-five cents!"

Chapter Eight

Lou's head snapped up. Twenty-five cents? She stood on tiptoe to see who had bid on her basket. Unfortunately it seemed everyone but Tommy Beasley was taller than she.

Marcy's voice said, "You sure, Hex?"

Hex Goolens? Hex had bid on her basket? A tidal wave of pleasure rushed through her. How sweet of him to come to her rescue!

"No, he's not sure!" a female voice called out.

Lou's heart sank as she spied Mrs. Goolens dragging Hex away by his ear. She swallowed hard over a sudden lump in her throat. She glared at Alex. This is what she had feared! Humiliation colored her face, clenched her fists, and had her biting her tongue to keep from saying something truly awful to her sister.

At the front of the crowd, Marcy hesitated. "This is, er, rather odd. Do I hear another bid? A nickel?"

This was too much to bear. Lou turned, prepared to walk back to the *Amazing Grace* if need be. She was leaving, with or without the rest of her family.

"One dollar."

The voice stopped her in her tracks. She looked across

the field at John. He didn't look at her, or even have a smile on his face. In fact, he looked angry.

Marcy stammered. "One dollar to Reverend Hewitt. Any other bidders?" She looked around, raised her hammer. "Going, going—"

"Two dollars!"

All heads turned. Hank Burnett stood on the edge of the crowd looking mighty determined. Lou looked back at John. He'd taken a step closer to her, and she saw the fierceness of his gaze.

He said, "Two-fifty."

"Three," Hank countered.

"Four."

"Five."

John was next to her now, standing over her as if protecting her. She wanted to lean into him, to feel his warmth. Yet she stepped away. He was putting his reputation on the line by bidding on her basket, and she was determined not to do anything that would embarrass him.

"Six."

Lou heard the hesitation in his voice as John said the number. She studied him carefully and saw an inner battle being fought through his eyes, and she suddenly realized why.

No furnishings in his house, threadbare clothes, and no hat to shade his face.

John Hewitt had little, or no, money at all.

Hank shuffled closer. The crowd formed a circle around them. "Seven."

"Eight," John said through clenched teeth.

Lou couldn't let him do this. Eight dollars was a fortune to a man who couldn't afford a hat. She placed her hand on his arm, and ignored the gasp that went through the crowd. "John, stop."

He shook his head. "No."

Hank rocked back on his heels. "Nine."

"Please stop, John. Please. The basket's not worth it. A couple of chicken pieces are not worth nine dollars."

He looked at her, stared at her with those blue eyes of his, and she saw the urgency in his gaze. "Let it be, Lou."

The crowd edged in. Tears clouded her eyes. "Your reputation . . ." she pleaded softly.

The sun shone off his dark hair. His eyes darkened. "Some things are more important, Lou. Ten dollars!"

Lou looked around at the spellbound faces. She turned to her family, hoping for help of some sort, but they were not to be seen.

Lou turned to Hank. Gone was his usually impassive expression, replaced now with one of complete intensity. She had the uneasy feeling there was more going on between Hank and John than bidding on a basket, yet she couldn't fathom what that might be.

As Hank took a deep breath, she held hers, waiting for the next impossible number to come out of his mouth. But none came. After a long moment, he bowed and disappeared into the crowd.

Marcy called out, "Ten dollars. Going, going, gone! Sold to Reverend Hewitt." She smiled. "You may pay up front and collect your basket."

Lou didn't miss the color draining from John's face as he realized he just purchased a fifty-cent lunch for ten dollars. Ten dollars he undoubtedly didn't have.

In a blink, his expression changed and a smile bloomed on his face. He crooked his elbow and she locked arms with him.

He stepped up to the table and pulled a money clip from his pocket. He pulled the sole ten dollar bill from his clip and handed it over to Marcy.

"What would you have done if Hank bid eleven?" Lou asked.

He smiled at her. "Wrote an IOU for twelve. Now, let's eat."

"The lunch really isn't worth it, John."

"You're right, Lou, it's not." He smiled. "But having you all to myself this afternoon is."

John shuffled the papers on his desk. The picnic, in his most solemn opinion, had not gone all that well. Yes, money had been raised for the church's coffers, and lunch with Lou had been delightful, especially when he learned she hadn't made it. And his pleasure had tripled when he learned that the repairs on the *Amazing Grace* had been completed. Hank would be out of Lou's life forever.

However, the baseball game had been a nightmare.

He shook his head, remembering. The Parkers had been more skilled than he thought, even playing short-handed since no one wanted to join their team. Or rather, Hex and all the others were denied permission to join their team.

He ground his teeth. What would it take to get the people of this town to accept the Parkers? Actually, he knew the answer to that particular question. Her name was Mrs. Leona Farrell. After what Levi had told him, he had a new understanding of the woman's hatred toward the Parkers, but to hold the grudge this long, and toward those innocent women who had nothing to do with their father's behavior, was unthinkable. Yet, it remained.

Thrived, even.

He breathed in deeply and Dog snuffled in his sleep. John had hated to leave him home during the picnic, but knowing Dog's feelings towards strangers, he felt it the best decision. Dog, however, hadn't felt that way and had gnawed on John's oak desk chair until it resembled tattered wicker.

Bending down, John rubbed Dog's head, his thoughts still churning about the Parkers and Mrs. Farrell. All day long he'd had the feeling others in his parish welcomed the inclusion of the Parkers. People like Levi and Hannah O'Grady. Hex Goolens and the other boys too. However, it had been Mrs. Farrell's watchful eye that made them keep their distance, and he couldn't precisely blame them.

Along with her inn, Mrs. Farrell also owned the only bank in town. She held power over the people of River Glen. Too much power, John reflected. To cross her would put in jeopardy the loans that kept their businesses afloat, their families fed.

If only he could get through to her.

A sharp knock on the front door echoed down the hallway and into the study. He started for the door before he remembered Cora had yet to leave for the night.

He shook his head as he remembered Lou asking him to take her on. He knew Lou Parker was going to send him to the poorhouse, yet he hadn't the willpower to deny her request of taking Cora in.

Cora pushed open the door to the study and stuck her curly head inside. Dog's tail thumped a happy rhythm.

"Who's here?" John asked. He didn't like the expression on her face, one that held more than a hint of anger.

"Too many to name, Reverend. I do believe it's your church council. I put them in the parlor."

He bit back a smile. There was nowhere to sit in the parlor.

"I'd best go see what they want."

Cora called to Dog, who followed her happily. "It ain't good news."

"How do you know?"

Shaking her head, she said, "With that bunch, it never is."

John took a calming breath as he walked down the hallway and stepped into the parlor.

"We need to see about getting you some furniture, Reverend," Levi Mason said.

John nodded as he took in the solemn faces, most of which wouldn't look him in the eye. Bad news indeed.

He folded his arms across his chest and looked to Mrs. Farrell. "What's this about?"

"I'll not beat around the bush, Reverend. Your behavior today shocked and embarrassed me. All of us, I daresay."

John looked around at Levi; at Hannah O'Grady; at George Cole, the butcher; at Adam Clark, the local grocer. "Is this true?"

None would look at him.

Mrs. Farrell thumped her cane. "Of course it's true! Do you accuse me of lying?"

"Never. Why, that would be sinful, would it not?"

"Don't sass me, young man."

Levi shuffled his foot. "Leona, you aren't making this easier."

John breathed deep. "What exactly is this, and how does it pertain to the Parkers?"

"The *Amazing Grace* is due to leave Cincinnati come Saturday for a two-week journey to St. Louis and back."

"I'm well aware of that, but what does it have to do with me?"

Mrs. Farrell fished in her large reticule. John was coming to hate that purse. She pushed a slip of paper into his hand. He stared at it in disbelief. "What is this?"

"It's your ticket to board that floating Gomorrah."

A headache thrummed behind his eyes. "Why?"

Snorting, Mrs. Farrell said, "There is wrongdoing happening aboard that boat and you're just the man to document it for us."

"What!"

"Those girls trust you. You'll be able to examine that boat stem to stern without being questioned."

Anger burned deep in him. "And what precisely am I looking for?"

"Evidence of their whoring. Once we have it, the sheriff will be called."

His fist clenched, crumpling the paper. "Whoring?" he repeated, the word coming out in a low hiss.

Mrs. Farrell crossed her arms over her chest. "That's right. Not to mention other sins."

John held up his hands to stop her before she could list them. "Do you all agree with this?"

"Of course they do," Mrs. Farrell snapped. "Don't you, Mrs. O'Grady?"

John sought Hannah's eyes. Hers were full of shame. His heart broke for her, knowing that she, as a widow, depended on Mrs. Farrell's loan to run her restaurant. Her agreement trembled off her lips.

John stood his ground. "I won't do it."

"You will."

He guided Mrs. Farrell to his front door. "My dear woman," he said through clenched teeth, "I do believe you're not feeling well. Invasive hatred in one's soul can do that to a person." A flicker of shame shot across her eyes and disappeared as quickly as it had come. "Might I suggest you go home and rest?"

Her eyes blazed. "I will have your resignation immediately."

His pulse thundered to a stop as the wind was knocked out of him with her words. He couldn't lose this job. It was all he had left. Yet, he knew this was a time to stand his ground. "Only my superiors have the power to fire me, Mrs. Farrell. And I think I asked you to leave."

Mrs. Farrell pressed her point. "We, as the church council, can petition for your release. Don't think we won't. How much do you like your job?"

Job? This wasn't a job to him. It was his whole life. He'd given up so much for what he believed in. . . .

Anger bubbled up. "Get out."

Mrs. Farrell stuck her many chins in the air and stomped out, slamming the front door behind her.

"All of you can leave now." John watched as they all filed out, eyes downcast. Levi, the last in line, paused at the door.

"Mebbe, I c'n have a word with you, Reverend?"

John stepped onto the porch, realizing he still held the ticket for the *Amazing Grace*. How had it come to this? How could Mrs. Farrell be so single minded?

"You can't actually agree with her, Levi." It was a trial to force the words past the angry lump lodged in his throat.

"Do I think the Parkers are as she paints 'em? Nah. They're good girls." He shook his head. "But I've got a business to run, Reverend. I can't be disagreeing with her now."

John shoved his clenched fists into his pockets. "Her power over the lot of you is wrong. Just plain wrong."

"We know it, but there ain't nothing we can do about it."

"Maybe not, but there's something I can do about it."

"What's that?"

John turned anguished eyes toward the old man. "Beat her at her own game."

"How?"

John rocked on his heels, a smile curving his lips. "No one will know what I do aboard that boat. Let Mrs. Farrell believe I'm investigating, when in fact I'll be gathering evidence to exonerate the Parkers once and for all." A whole two weeks to spend with Lou away from prying eyes. "But I'll need your help, Levi." He explained his hopes.

"So, while you're a-cruisin', I'll be working on Mrs. Farrell to put the past where it belongs?" He scratched at his beard. "It might work. It's long past time, Reverend."

John held out his hand. Levi clasped it firmly. "You don't be doing nothin' I wouldn't do on that boat."

As Levi walked down the steps, John asked, "And what would that be?"

Levi guffawed. "Not much."

John watched as he climbed into the wagon, the others waiting for him, none looking John in the eye. Except Mrs. Farrell.

"What's it going to be, Reverend?"

John bit back a grin at his devilish plan. "When's the boat due to leave?"

"Saturday next," she answered.

"I'll be on it."

"I'm glad you've come to see things my way, Reverend."

Plumes of dust remained in the council members' wake as Levi's parting words echoed in John's head.

You don't be doing nothin' I wouldn't do on that boat.

After closing the front door, he leaned against it. It was one thing to convince the town to accept the Parkers, and an entirely different matter to convince them to accept that he was courting Lou. He was going to have two weeks with her. Two weeks he'd use to figure out if he was truly falling in love with her.

And two weeks to figure out what to do about it.

Chapter Nine

Lou fairly skipped down the *Amazing Grace*'s hallway. Today was the day for which they had all been waiting. Their maiden voyage.

Not precisely, but close enough.

It was the *Amazing Grace*'s maiden voyage as a hotel, and the changes were remarkable. The Hurricane Deck, below the pilothouse, held two dining rooms, a ballroom, crew quarters, and some passenger quarters. The Texas Deck held passenger quarters, the Gentlemen's Lounge, and the Gaming Hall. The old cargo hold was now the Main Deck and lobby of the *Amazing Grace*. Along with the boilers, it held boutiques, a small general store, a barbershop, and activity centers for the children aboard, including a small theater.

Two weeks on the river. Two weeks of being Madame Angelique . . .

She paused at the end of the hallway and looked starboard, toward yet another hallway. This one led to suites of staterooms meant for families. The old threadbare rug had been replaced with thick, forest-green carpet shipped in from Georgia. One side of the hall had been papered a soft, watery, moss green, and one of the workmen, talented with an art brush, had painted a beautiful mural on one side along the hall. It was a majestic picture of the new *Amazing Grace* floating along the river, black clouds trailing from the smoke stacks behind her.

Lou's pulse thrummed in her ear as she stared at the serene mural. The picture made it seem as though every-thing was all right in her small existence when she knew it was not.

She'd not had a chance to say good-bye to John. In fact, with the preparation of the boat's departure, she had not seen him since their picnic.

She gnawed her lower lip, feeling the smile that trembled there. The picnic had been lovely. Truly lovely.

The baseball game . . . had not been.

All in all, she had to thank Alex for forcing her to go. However, a small part of her also despaired, knowing that it would have been much wiser to have remained home.

Reaching out, she traced her fingers over the wisps of smoke trailing behind the *Amazing Grace* in the mural.

"It's lovely."

Lou spun around, her hand flying to her heart. "Hank!"

"Did I frighten you?"

He had. "I didn't hear you behind me." She spied a valise sitting at his feet, and looked at him questioningly.

He shifted his long, lanky body from foot to foot. "I thought to enjoy a bit of a vacation."

He seemed different, somehow. Then she realized he'd stopped stuttering around her. Her thoughts swirled as she tried to remember. The vocal tic had stopped after he caught her lying on top of John.

Oh, what he must think of her!

Her cheeks flamed. "I'm sure the *Amazing Grace* will provide you with a great amount of relaxation, Hank."

Stepping nearer, he said, "I truly look forward to seeing

Madame Angelique perform. I've heard her rehearse while I worked. Her voice is truly quite lovely. Truly." His hard, silver-blue gaze bore into her.

Surely, he did not know! Did he? He couldn't! She twisted her hands and turned back to the mural.

Gone was the sense of peace the picture had elicited.

Her voice cracked. "Have you met Madame Angelique?"

He stepped beside her, the sleeve of his suit coat brushing her shoulder.

"No, I haven't had the pleasure."

She longed to step aside, to excuse herself, but guilt held her in place. She owed Hank Burnett what was left of her reputation and all of John's. As far as she knew, he hadn't told anyone what he witnessed that day in John's yard.

Forcing herself to be still, she remained where she was. "Truly lovely."

She met his gaze that hadn't left her face. She swallowed.

"The artwork?" he said.

Oh! Of course he had been talking about the mural. How silly of her. "Yes, it's lovely."

"So peaceful."

That had been her first reaction to the painting as well. Now, however, her nerves had twisted into painful knots. Her palms were damp as she wrung her hands.

She cast a longing glance down the empty hallway. Could she excuse herself without seeming rude?

"I—" she began.

"Lou—" he said.

She smiled. "You first."

His huge hands clutched her wrists. "Lou." Those hard eyes stared at her with such intensity. She wished someone would walk around the corner. Anyone. Just so she wouldn't feel so alone.

"Y-yes?"

He towered over her, making her feel small and helpless. "Would you do me the honor of dining with me tonight?"

It was on the tip of her tongue to decline. She surely wouldn't be able to eat a bite of food with him hovering so close to her. However, she did appreciate all he had done for her. For John.

Dinner was the least she could offer to show her gratitude. His hands slipped from her wrists and engulfed her tiny fists.

However, if his attentions continued, she would have to speak with him. Tell him that they should remain friends and nothing more.

"I'll meet you in the dining room at eight," she said.

He didn't release her hands, not even at her gentle tugging. Her damp palms betrayed her nervousness. Surely he noticed? "I'll pick you up at your room."

Gently, she shook her head. Again she tugged on her hands, yet they remained captive. Hard calluses abraded her skin. "No. No, thank you. It's not necessary."

"Truly, I don't mind."

Lou breathed a sigh of relief as footsteps echoed down the hall. Someone was coming.

Tipping her head, she forced a smile past her parched lips. "You're very kind, Hank, but I'd rather—"

"Lou?"

Happiness filled her at the sound of her name spoken in John's voice. Her spirits were buoyed. "John?"

John's eyes had narrowed on her hands. "Have I interrupted something?"

"No," she said, never so happy to admit the truth in her whole life.

"Yes," said Hank.

The malice in Hank's tone disturbed her. She gave a forceful yank on her hands and Hank finally released them.

"Hank and I were finished with our conversation."

Tension crackled between the two men. She stepped between them.

She took John's hand. His touch offered her warmth, a calmness that drew her to him. "What are you doing here?"

"I came to find you."

"To say good-bye?"

He smiled wide and bright. Her heart tumbled. "To say hello. I've come to ask you to dinner."

Confusion swept through her. "But we back out of the Landing in an hour."

"Yes, I know. I've booked passage."

Her eyes widened with her delighted smile. She fairly bounced with excitement. "How wonderful!"

His heady blue gaze turned tender as it narrowed on her face. His voice dropped a bit as he said, "Might you care to join me for dinner?"

Oh, there was nothing she'd rather do!

She felt John stiffen and followed his gaze over her shoulder. Hank! She had forgotten he stood there. Her smile faltered.

"I'm sorry, John." And she was. "I already have plans."

Lou descended the stairs into the main lobby in search of one of her sisters. She was in dire need of advice and had no one else to turn to.

The lobby was filled with people browsing through the shops. Luckily, Matt and Alex had hired many extra hands to help with the transition of the boat, even daring to woo the best of Cincinnati's hotel employees from their employers, so everything was running quite smoothly.

After greeting several couples who were checking in, Lou found Jack nose-to-nose with a very elegant, very uptight older woman.

"I'm sorry, ma'am," Jack was saying.

The woman's aristocratic nose shot into the air. "But as I've said, I wish to board."

The warning whistle rang out, alerting passengers that the stage would soon raise. Excitement shuddered through Lou. In another hour, the *Amazing Grace* would be floating down the Ohio. Her excitement, however, was tempered by Jack's frustration.

She watched her sister's fingers curl into a fist and stepped in. "Jack? Is something wrong?"

Before Jack could answer, the formidable woman said, "I am Eloisa Scranton Regent of the New York City Regents. Surely you've heard of us?"

Indeed she had; who hadn't? The Regent name was synonymous with Rockefeller in terms of wealth and position. How had this woman found her way to their little corner of Ohio?

Jack's blue eyes flashed fire. "I have told Mrs. Eloisa Scranton Regent that there are no more rooms available, but she insists I find one."

Lou eyed the woman in all her stylish refinery. A part of her longed to be able to carry off such an outfit, such an attitude. From hat to shoes, the woman was the picture of everything Lou had ever admired.

Smiling, Lou said, "I will take care of it."

Jack's fingers unfurled. "How?"

"I will think of something."

To Mrs. Scranton Regent, Lou said, "Come with me. My name is Lou Parker." She linked arms with the older woman. "Please forgive my sister. Her temper has been short since her beau left town to take care of family matters. Not that he, precisely, is her beau. . . ." Lou frowned, realizing she was rambling. "Please excuse my manners."

"No, no, do go on. I do so love matters of the heart."

Lou leaned in conspiratorially. "I believe she loves him."

"Oh my."

"However, I don't think she realizes it as yet."

With a heavy sigh, Mrs. Scranton Regent murmured, "Time will release all secrets."

Lou hoped not. She had many she never wanted revealed. "Are you newly arrived in Cincinnati?"

"Indeed. I arrived via train from New York City just this morning."

"You must be exhausted!"

"Only on the inside, dear."

"Pardon?"

A large feathered hat shaded the woman's face, but sadness etched every line creasing her eyes and mouth. "Like your sister, I too am heartbroken. I've come to Ohio to mend old hurts, and to hopefully restore a bond hastily broken. Which is why I need passage aboard the *Amazing Grace*, Miss Parker. I arrived in town to learn that the person I seek is aboard."

"Did this person know of your arrival?"

She squeezed Lou's hand. "No. I thought to surprise him. However, I am not sure he will even speak with me. He is very angry."

Sympathy flowed through Lou. How awful for this woman. "As my sister said, there are simply no rooms remaining."

All the vibrant life in the woman seemed to seep out. Her shoulders slumped.

"However, I will surrender my own room and stay with my sister. The room is not overly spacious, but it is tidy," Lou smiled with good humor, "and aboard the boat."

For a moment Mrs. Scranton Regent said nothing. When she finally spoke, her eyes shimmered. "I've never known such kindness, Miss Parker, without paying for it. I do not know what to say."

Lou patted her arm. "First of all, please call me Lou." She worried her lip. Before her was the very type of woman who would appeal to River Glen society. The mannerisms, the clothing, the air of dignity. Perhaps she could persuade Mrs. Scranton Regent to be her mentor, just for the night. She would seek John out after her supper with Hank. She longed to show John that she was willing to change to fit his world. Perhaps then they could move forward with a true courtship.

Mrs. Scranton Regent arched an eyebrow. "And secondly?"

"There is a matter of heart at hand for myself as well. A man whom I care for deeply."

"Does he return the sentiment?"

"To a certain degree, I believe."

Warily, Mrs. Scranton Regent asked, "What is it you wish me to do?"

"It will cost you nothing but your time, ma'am." Lou gestured to her clothes, her hair, and leaned in to whisper in her ear.

A smile spread across Mrs. Scranton Regent's face. "My dear, I'd be delighted."

Chapter Ten

John stepped into the dining room, where crystal chandeliers above were twinkling with candlelight. Modern electric lights hid behind silver sconces along the wall cast a soft glow upwards.

He tugged at his dinner jacket and looked about the room for Lou. He needed to speak to her. Immediately. He'd spent most of the afternoon searching the boat for her with little luck. Once, he had spotted her deep in conversation with an older woman whose large hat had hidden her own face and most of Lou's. They'd looked so serious, he'd decided not to interrupt.

Scanning past the linen-covered tables, his gaze skipped from face to face. As he suspected, she wasn't here. If she had been, his nerves would have been pulled taut, as they were wont to do whenever she was close. It was the most discomfiting sensation, yet at the same time he didn't want to be rid of it.

She made him feel alive. Whole. She liked him for who he was, not for his family name since she knew none of his background. She brought a joy to his life like he had never known, and he never wanted to experience life without her in it.

Hank Burnett sidled up to him. "Reverend."

"Hank."

Hank pulled out his pocket watch. "Lou is running late."

John bit his lip and rocked on his heels.

As if intent on baiting him, Hank said, "She's truly lovely."

"Yes, she is." Disgust ate at John. Images of the day several months before came swiftly to him. Hank, crying, pleading to be absolved of guilt. He'd told John about the years he'd spent in a Colorado prison—years his family and neighbors thought he was traveling west. Years of punishment for hurting women in the most vile way possible.

It had turned John's stomach just hearing of the crimes, but fear had scampered up his spine when Hank admitted that he wasn't sure he could control his base urges.

Now, he was having dinner with an unsuspecting Lou.

Over John's dead body.

A wine glass clinked nearby. "You need to stay away from the Parkers, Hank."

Hank clapped John on the back. "No need to worry, Reverend."

John turned to face him. "Aren't you worried about keeping restraint?" he said tightly.

"I'm fine. Truly fine. Never been better."

This couldn't go on. John had to do something to prevent something terrible from happening.

"You're not thinking of saying something, are you, Reverend? I'm not sure that God would forgive you breaking the confidences of the collar."

John couldn't believe what he was hearing. Was Hank threatening *him*?

Hank's beady eyes narrowed. "If you mention my past,

Reverend, I might have to say something too. About a certain scene I witnessed not too long—"

John grabbed Hank's lapels and pushed him out into the hallway. He shoved him against a wall. "I am not some defenseless woman you can intimidate, Hank." Hank's eyes darkened. "You will stay away from the Parkers, or word will get out about your past. If it ruins my reputation as a minister, then so be it. At least I will have a clear conscience."

John backed off and smoothed Hank's coat. "Have I made myself clear?"

"Gentlemen?"

John turned in tandem with Hank at the sound of Lou's voice. His jaw dropped. "Lou?"

Her chin was down, and a blush colored her ears, her cheeks. Her hair lay piled atop her head in delicate curls. She wore a pale green evening dress, cut low at her creamy throat. Her bare shoulders shone under the glow of the sconce above her head. She turned slightly and his breath caught as he saw that the back of the dress scooped down, the gentle folds providing little coverage of her pale skin. The skirt of the dress pinched her tiny waist and billowed slightly at her ankles as she stepped toward them.

"Is something wrong here?" she asked.

Hank's mouth hung open. John frowned. She didn't need to be adding fuel to Hank's desire by parading around in something so . . . so breathtaking.

"Yes," he said, "there is something wrong." He grabbed hold of Lou's elbow and guided her forcefully toward a set of double doors leading to a balcony.

Her eyes clouded with confusion and hurt as she looked up at him, but he was too upset to notice.

He heard footsteps behind him and he stopped short, jerking Lou up beside him protectively. He turned to Hank. "I strongly suggest you stay here."

Hank looked at Lou.

Her gaze dropped to John's hand, still latched around her elbow. Through tightly clenched teeth, she said, "It's okay, Hank."

She pulled her arm out of John's grasp, picked up the hem of her gown, and stomped off.

John followed her as she dashed through a set of thick French doors to a balcony overlooking the churning Ohio River.

Small lights along the railing highlighted her flushed face. She shot a fiery look his way when he reached her side. Before he could even think about apologizing, she reared back and kicked him in the shin.

He danced around on one foot, which smarted from the pain.

Anger came off her in waves. "Do you care to explain yourself?"

John immediately felt remorseful for his brutish behavior. It hadn't been his intention to hurt her . . . he simply wanted to get her away from Hank.

Her voice shook. "Have you nothing to say for yourself?"

Rubbing his shin, he tried to think of a way he could make it up to her, to ease her anger while he fought to find a way to explain himself. He could think of no words. And the longer he watched the heat flicker and flare in her violet eyes, the more he needed to touch her, to soothe her.

He took a step nearer and she turned away, looking out at the river as it trailed behind them.

With the decking vibrating beneath his feet, he slipped behind her, bracketing her with his arms. He leaned his head against her curls and breathed in the scent of lilacs. "I'm sorry."

She ducked under his arm. "I need more than an apology,

John." Confusion flickered in her eyes. "What happened back there?"

The side wheel paddles, enclosed in decorative boxes, cut through the murky water. The sound of splashing water echoed through the still night. Lou grasped the railing, her knuckles white, as she stared at him, waiting.

"I'm sorry," he said again. Why could he think of nothing else to say? Because he surely couldn't tell her the truth. That Hank preyed on innocents like herself. That, and John wanted to be alone with her, to finally admit how he felt.

It was highly unlikely she would listen now.

Moisture pooled in her eyes. "Don't you like the gown?"

Pain stabbed him in his chest. He'd done this to her, made her doubt herself, her beauty. He was the worst kind of louse, and he silently cursed himself. "You look lovely, Lou, but then, you always do." He drew in a deep breath. "You were perfect the way you were. Why the change?"

The fire crept out of her eyes. She looked uncertain, vulnerable. The moon crept up over the horizon and settled in the dark, starless sky.

Her chin tipped up and a rush of admiration filled him. Her soft, mellifluous voice held a tight edge as she said, "I wanted to be respectable."

The steamboat shuddered as it slowed around a bend. Above his head, dark smoke from the stacks blended into the inky night. He curved his palm over her petal-soft cheek. "You don't need a pretty dress to be respectable. You've always been respectable."

She pressed her cheek into his palm, causing an ache behind his ribs. "Not everyone thinks so."

His thumb began to make a circle. "Have I ever treated you otherwise?"

Wide violet eyes stared up at him. She blinked and looked away. "You've been nothing but kind."

She moved away from his touch. His hand curled into a fist to capture the warmth left behind. "What is this truly about, Lou?"

With a loud sigh, she sat on a bench. "I thought . . ."

He sat next to her and murmured in her ear. "What?"

She shivered despite the warm night. "I thought a change of wardrobe might boost my respectability." She gazed up at him. "Not only in your eyes, but your congregation's eyes." She threw her hands into the air. "I thought that if I acted like a lady, was seen like a lady, they would treat me like a lady."

Swiftly, anger coursed through him. He took hold of her hands, forcing her complete attention. "I have never met more of a lady in my whole life. Your bright soul shines through everything you do. Everyday, you brighten others' lives just by being you. Your smile, your free spirit, your joy of life."

She looked uncertain. "Do—do you really believe so?"

He tipped her chin. "I know so."

"Do you want to know the saddest part of this all?"

"What's that?"

She picked up her skirt and let it fall in a gentle puddle around her ankles. "I like dresses, always have. Jack and Alex were perfectly content with their styles, but I, because I was so ill, spent more time with our mother who enjoyed reading of the latest fashions in Godey's Lady's Book. I suppose I absorbed it as well."

"Did you ever tell your father you wished to wear dresses?"

She shook her head. "No."

"Why not?"

Her delicate shoulders arched in a shrug. "We simply didn't talk back to Father."

"But he's been gone now for many months. Why not then?"

Tipping her head, she stared out over the river before turning her amazing eyes on him. "Truth be told, I enjoy wearing pants too. They offer women a freedom nothing else can. And beyond that, I never knew what to wear. Or what style would look right on me, or even how to style my hair with curling tongs."

"You certainly did a fine job tonight. You look beautiful."

Her smile turned impish. "I had help."

"From whom?"

She smiled that luminescent, mischievous smile he loved. "My fairy godmother."

The moon disappeared behind a cloud. "Godmother or not, you should wear whatever you wish whenever you want."

She traced the line of his jaw with her fingertips, sending a jolt of awareness up his spine. "Now that I've shared one of my secrets with you, you must share on of yours." Her fingers curled away from his face as her hand dropped to her lap. "Why were you and Hank arguing, John?"

Lou held her breath. Would he tell her the truth, or once again change the subject? First Dog, then Daphne, now John . . . All held Hank in contempt. Why?

"It's very long and complicated."

"Oh."

She had hoped it would be something simple, but had suspected by his demeanor that it was not. "So you won't tell me."

His lips tightened as he frowned. "I wish I could, Lou."

"Then it isn't—" She broke off, unable to believe what she had been about to ask.

"Is it what?"

She rose, her gown falling around her ankles. She loved the feel of the silk against her skin. Mrs. Scranton Regent had loved the boutique aboard the *Amazing Grace*. In fact she had chosen quite a few dresses that would compliment Lou's coloring, but Lou had fallen in love with this one. With its dramatic lines and sheer elegance, it had been exactly what she hoped to turn John's head.

And it had. Just not in the way she'd daydreamed about.

John came up behind her, and she wished he'd once again lay his cheek on her head, slide his hands down her arms, but he didn't touch her. "What were you going to say, Lou?"

"It's nothing."

He tipped her chin upward so she'd look at him. The dark night turned his blue eyes black. It was impossible to tell where the pupil met the iris.

"I think," he said softly, "that it's time we started being honest with each other."

She bit back a cry of frustration. Honest. It was the one thing she couldn't be with him. Their relationship was a tender one, not exactly courting, not exactly not. He thought she was a lady, and she didn't want to shatter that image of her. If he ever found out she was Madame Angelique, she would lose him forever. Because she knew he couldn't sacrifice his calling, or his reputation, for her, and she wouldn't want him to.

She felt it necessary to at least tell him a bit of the truth. "Don't we all have things we keep to ourselves? Secrets best left alone?"

"Everyone has secrets, Lou." A warm spring breeze ruffled his hair.

"Even you?"

"Even me."

She couldn't possibly imagine what secrets a reverend could possess.

He tucked a wayward curl behind her ear. "But there's one thing I don't want to keep secret any longer."

His finger lingered behind her ear. Slow caresses that had her pulse pounding, her stomach churning, and a heat settling over her from head to toe. Slightly out of breath, she asked, "What's that?"

His head inched lower. His hand sank into her curls. "My feelings for you."

Her breath hitched as his lips settled on hers, warm and searching. She let go of the railing, leaning in to meet his kiss, adoring the way his touch made her feel. Weak yet strong. Desirable. Loved.

His hand drifted to her back, his fingers making lazy sweeps of her skin. After a moment he pulled away, his breath coming in ragged bursts.

He leaned his forehead against hers. She fought the impulse to reach for him again, knowing it would be most improper, and improper was the last thing she wanted to be.

John said, "I'd like, very much, Lou Parker, if you would have dinner with me, tonight and every night we're aboard this boat."

Her smile faltered. "But what of your congregation? They will not approve."

He took her elbow and led her to the set of double doors leading to the dining room. "Let me worry about them."

She wished she could. It was one thing for the town to accept her as a Parker, but she had heard the rumors around town of Madame Angelique's reputation. Fallen. Whore. Jezebel. She swallowed hard. She could never prove the rumors false unless she confessed who was really behind the singer's mask. And even then, she feared the accusations cast upon Madame Angelique would be thrown her way.

Madame Angelique! She'd forgotten!

"What time is it?" Lou asked John, her heart in her throat. Her first night singing and she had forgotten!

He pulled out a tarnished watch fob. "Shortly after nine."

"I've got to go." She picked up her hem and dashed down the hallway.

"Lou?" John called behind her.

"Good-bye!"

She pushed through a set of swinging doors at the end of the hallway, excitement pulsing through her at what was to come that night onstage, and the memory of John's kiss still lingering on her lips.

Chapter Eleven

"**W**here do you disappear every night?" John asked, taking the picnic basket out of her hand.

The night she'd left him standing on the Hurricane Deck, nearly a week ago, she'd barely had enough time even with Daphne's help to change into her costume before the curtain swung open for Madame Angelique's debut performance. She felt lighter than a feather as she remembered the applause and whistles.

"Lou?"

She gnawed her lower lip. "Helping Jack." She bit out the lie, hating herself for keeping the truth from him.

The lobby doors opened into the brilliant sunshine, and Lou's smile widened. It seemed as though all her dreams were coming true.

"Why are you smiling?"

"I was thinking of you, of course."

He linked his free hand through her elbow. He grinned. "Of course. Where are we off to?"

The *Amazing Grace* had docked in Canoe Falls, just outside St. Louis, for an afternoon of freedom for the passengers. Matt predicted they would reach St. Louis the following evening. "Matt told me the river bends about a half mile up. It should be a lovely place for a picnic."

Dozens of steamboat passengers roamed the streets, their feet kicking up dust, their boot heels clattering on the wooden walkways lining both sides of the road.

Lou stopped as she spotted Mrs. Scranton Regent peering into the window of a shoe shop. When she looked up, Lou waved. The older woman's eyes went wide under the brim of her enormous hat as she hesitantly lifted her own hand in return.

John stopped short, and Lou stumbled. He caught her before she fell, and when Lou looked up, Mrs. Scranton Regent was gone.

"What's wrong?" she asked John. The color had drained from his face.

Looking her way, he seemed to not see her at all. She snapped her fingers in front of his face.

He blinked and shook his head. "I thought I saw someone I knew from a long time ago."

"Who?"

"No one. It's impossible. I must be seeing things."

Lou wondered at his abrupt change in manner. Something, or someone, had spooked him. She looked over her shoulder as they walked down the street, wondering just who it could have been.

"Have you been here before?" he asked, his voice still slightly shaken.

"No, I haven't. Have you?"

"Not to this town, but to St. Louis. My father took me there when I was ten or so."

"How exciting."

"I suppose it was."

"You suppose?"

"My father is a very . . . hard man."

A well-worn path guided their way. "How so?"

"I've disappointed him many times with my life choices."

She stopped to look at his face. Pain lingered in his dark blue eyes. "Surely he could hold nothing wrong with you becoming a man of the cloth?"

He nudged her forward. "He could, and he did."

"How terrible. Is that why you don't go back to New York?"

"One of the reasons."

Several large boulders blocked the path. John took her hand and guided her over them. For a week now they'd spent nearly every minute together, learning about each other, laughing, and for Lou, falling in love. Yet she knew nothing about his family, his past. Whenever she brought it up, he changed the subject.

Longing to know more about him, she said, "Surely your grandmother didn't cast you out as well?"

"She never spoke her feelings one way or another."

She turned, seeking his eyes. "Have you ever thought of returning? Of making amends? John, they're your family."

Eyebrows dipped, he frowned. "Not anymore. My congregation is my family now."

Lou shuddered at the thought of having Mrs. Farrell as a relative.

"They need me more than my family ever will, or ever had, for that matter."

Her fingers settled on his chin. She knew how it felt to be in disfavor with a parent. She let the issue be. John would have to come to terms with his family on his own.

A breeze ruffled his dark hair. She smiled up at him. "Come on, let's go eat."

The path widened into a sandy expanse. Several trees and thick underbrush formed a horseshoe-shaped alcove. The river's edge lapped peacefully onto the sandy shore that was bracketed with thick reeds and tall grasses.

It was just the spot for which she hoped. She sat in the sun-warmed sand and took off her boots.

John set the basket down next to her. Looking up, she found him staring.

"It's beautiful," he said.

Blushing, she shaded her eyes. The sun shone bright overhead, its beams sparkling silver off the river's surface. A cardinal and its mate flew overhead. It felt as though magical things could happen here. She looked at him and blinked. "Very beautiful."

For a moment, they stared at one another. Lou's heart beat so loudly she was sure he could hear it. Afraid of looking like she wanted another kiss—which she most certainly did—she turned toward the water and dipped her toes in.

Behind her, she heard John pick up the basket and had to wonder what he was thinking. Did he long to kiss her too?

The scent of jasmine drew her from the water's edge over to the thicket of trees. She wrapped her arm around the trunk of the old beech, resting her head against its bark. Birds chattered and bees buzzed in her ears as John spread out the blanket.

With bated breath, she watched as he removed his shoes. As he wiggled his toes in the sand, she smiled, thinking of their conversation from the other night.

Everyone has secrets, Lou.

Even you?

Even me. But there's one thing I don't want to keep secret any longer.

What's that?

My feelings for you.

Everything would be fine, she said silently, and willed herself to believe it. She released the tree and walked about the small clearing, pausing to smell the wildflowers. She tucked a small daisy into her hair before settling onto the blanket next to him.

"Are you hungry?" she asked.

"Famished."

She watched as he opened the hamper and carefully inspected every morsel within, and had to laugh. "Do not worry. Daphne made it, not me."

"Thank the heavens above."

She tossed him a sour look. "My cooking is not all that bad."

Thickly-lashed eyes widened. "In comparison to what, may I ask?"

Drawing her lip into her mouth to keep from smiling, she said, "Swill? Slop?"

Pressing his finger to his chin, he looked as if he was in deep contemplation. "Not that I have ever sampled either, but I would say it would be close, for I *have* tasted your cooking."

Her mouth dropped open. "You're a wretch, John Hewitt."

He unwrapped a sandwich and passed it to her. "Indeed I am. Please, though, don't spread the word. As you know, a man of the cloth is supposed to be holy at all times."

Teasing, she said, "Your reputation will be forever sullied." As soon as the words left her mouth, her smile faltered.

"Please, Lou, don't even think it."

She picked at the corner of her egg sandwich and asked, her eyes wide, "Think what?"

"That innocent act might work on others, Lou, but I know you too well."

Oh, he did know her well. Too well at times, she feared. What would he do if he ever learned of her secret identity? She placed her sandwich on a cloth napkin. "I cannot help but feel that your congregation will not like our relation-ship."

Though John seemed to think there would be no reper-cussions on his life or his career if his relationship with her became known, she knew different. And now that she knew he thought of his congregation as family . . . She couldn't be the one to take that away from him. The guilt would be her undoing.

He squeezed her hand, and she tried to ignore the pound-ing of her heart as he said, "I'm trying hard to change their ways, Lou, to make them see that different is not bad, it's just different. They've lived their whole lives thinking a certain way. I need to go about it slowly."

"I know."

He moved closer to her. "They need to trust me. Who am I to them? I'm a young reverend, just out of the sem-inary. They're still skeptical of my qualifications."

"I know."

"Every other week the subject of my sermons is accep-tance. I try to disguise it with fancy words and Biblical stories, but it's there. One of these days they're going to hear it in their hearts."

Her temper rising, she said, "I know. I know all of that, John. But it doesn't change the fact—" Heavens, she'd al-most said it. *That I love you.* She nibbled her lip.

His blue gaze softened. "What? Doesn't change what?"

She shook her head. "Nothing." She couldn't say it. Not yet. She needed his congregation to accept her, her family. And that wasn't likely to happen anytime soon, despite John's hopes. Mrs. Farrell's hatred ran too deep.

"You're quite beautiful when you're angry. And lying," he said. "Care to confess your sins to the good reverend?"

"No, I do not. Besides, sometimes lying is for the best and shouldn't be considered a sin at all." She reached in the hamper and removed a bottle of lemonade.

He held out a cup. "Do you really think so?"

She looked up. His gaze searched hers. Would he think less of her because she had the tendency to tell white lies? At that moment she thought about lying to him, to raise his opinion of her, but couldn't bring herself to do it. "I do. If I hadn't lied to Matt about Alex's interest in him, they might not be married today."

"I seem to recall it was emotional blackmail that found Alex her husband."

Lou contemplated what he said. "That may have played a part. However," she held up her hand, "it turned out well in the end, did it not?"

"So a wrong makes a right?"

She narrowed her gaze on him. "Is this going to end up as a sermon?"

He smiled, the slight crinkles at the corners of his eyes lifting. "It just might."

"Then I refuse to involve myself further."

The cup hovered at his lips. "Wise idea." He pursed his lips after he took a sip of the lemonade and his face turned three shades of red.

Lou cringed. "You don't like it?"

He managed to swallow. When he spoke, his words came out as a squeak. "You made the lemonade, didn't you?"

Slowly, she nodded. "Didn't you like it?"

"If I were to ever need to die a quick death, it will be the first thing I request."

"Wretch."

He finished his sandwich. "Did you hear Madame Angelique sing last night?"

She stiffened, a piece of bread lodging in her throat. Choking, she reached for the lemonade. After taking a sip of the horrible drink, she looked at him, searching for any suspicion. "Yes, I did."

"Her voice is lovely."

Lou's eyes widened. "You were there?"

"Yes."

The lights had been too bright to see the faces in the rear of the room. She'd have to make sure the lights were dimmed from now on. "Did you enjoy the show?"

"It was marvelous. You did quite well in finding a songstress."

Could he hear her heartbeat? It sounded as loud as a blacksmith's hammer to her own ears. "Thank you," she murmured.

She stiffened as a twig snapped, then another. "Did you hear that?"

John was already on his feet. "Who's out there?" he called into the thicket.

When no one answered, John turned to her. "Stay here."

Barefooted, he dashed into the trees, his form quickly swallowed by the dense underbrush.

Had someone been watching them? Why? She winced as she realized she had been biting her lip so hard it bled. She spotted a splash of white in the darkness of the trees and recognized it as John's collar.

A fine sheen of sweat dampened his hair as he came out of the woods. Hair tousled, barefoot, and dressed in black, he looked like a dark angel.

"Find anything?" she asked.

"No."

"Who would be watching us?"

They sat on the blanket. Storminess glazed John's eyes. "I don't know."

He crumpled his napkin and tossed it into the basket. "Well, let's not have it ruin our afternoon."

"Agreed."

For a while they spoke of the things they wished to do upon arriving in St. Louis, and of her family, and of Dog, whom John missed greatly. However, it wasn't long before John's eyes had once again narrowed in concern.

"Did you see Hank this morning?" he asked.

"He asked me to dinner. I declined."

Was that relief in his eyes? "How did he react?"

"Quite well. Though I must speak to him soon."

"Why?"

"It's very simple, John. I don't want to lead Hank astray. He seems to harbor feelings for me, and I think it would be cruel to let him believe anything could ever come of them." Her voice dropped to a whisper. She looked at him through lowered lashes. "Because it's really no secret that my heart belongs to another."

There were so many qualities she admired about John, from his ability to look past people's flaws and see them for who they were—or at the very least, what they could become—to his gentle kindness shown in the way he treated others. How many times had he overlooked her bursts of temper, always offering his ear should she need someone to listen to? Too many to count.

Somewhere between playing baseball in the rain with him and his kiss, she had let her heart be influenced by his quiet strength, his moral character, and his complete acceptance of who she was and how she had been raised.

Unfortunately, beyond that kiss, she had no idea how he felt about her.

He tugged her to her feet, a smile lifting the corners of his mouth. "Would I know this person?"

She heard the tenderness in his voice. "I think so."

His thumb swept across her lips, but he didn't kiss her. "Please, promise me something."

"What?"

"Stay away from Hank, Lou."

Mouth agape, she stared. What was it between the two? "Why? Why, John?"

He tugged at his white collar as though it had suddenly become a noose. "It's just . . ." Shaking his head, he said, "Nothing."

If he had reason to want her to stay away from Hank, she would, even if he couldn't share it with her.

She sensed his inner turmoil and wanted to alleviate it. With a laugh meant to lighten his mood, she poked him in the chest. "Aha! A lie! From the sainted reverend too. 'Nothing,' " she mocked and tsked. "You shock me, John."

He couldn't believe his good fortune to have found such a woman. She was bright, funny, beautiful. He looked forward to her bursts of anger because they were honest and real, and they revealed emotions most people kept hidden from him. She simply liked him for who he was. And that was more than he could have ever wished.

His congregation would have to accept Lou and their relationship; there was no two ways about it. She had committed no sin, done nothing wrong—in the eyes of God or his congregation.

He wished he could relay to her what Levi had told him of Mrs. Farrell, but John felt the conversation should be kept in confidence. He hoped to heaven above Levi was making headway with Leona Farrell.

"John?"

Lou touched his chin, nudging it in her direction. He wanted to capture those fingers, press kisses to them, but he kept still. He feared if he touched her, he wouldn't be able to stop.

"I didn't mean to offend you," she said softly. "I was teasing."

He took hold of her hand and pulled it away from his face. "Of course you were. I was lost in thought for a moment."

"Nothing serious, I hope."

Fingers of sunlight pulsed through the branches over-head, lighting her blond hair, making it shine as though God himself had just touched her head. Her beauty was breathtaking, but it was her spirit, her soul, that had cap-tured his heart.

A crumb clung to her lip and he reached out and brushed it away, his thumb lingering.

Their gazes caught and held, and for a long time they said nothing as his heart drummed his ribs. He longed to take her in his arms, hold her tight, and kiss her long and hard—to show her with his touch what he feared to say aloud.

He loved her.

When it had happened he wasn't quite sure. There had been that instant connection the first time he'd met her, and from then on he'd been awed by her humor, her generosity, her humility.

Reluctantly, he pulled his hand back. "Serious? That de-pends on how you define the word." Given time, he hoped she would be his wife. She would be his to hold, to laugh with, to love.

"How cryptic. Are you purposely trying to arouse my curiosity?"

"Perhaps."

She shook her head. "One day, I will be your confessor and you can tell me all your worries."

She was one of a kind. And for now, she was his. "Some-day, I will."

"How about now?" she asked.

Her earlier words echoed back to him. *Besides, some-times lying is for the best and shouldn't be considered a sin at all.* This, he knew, was one of those times. "I prom-ise," he said.

"I'm going to hold you to that."

"I don't doubt it for a moment."

He followed as she danced to the water's edge, her face alight with a glorious smile.

She picked up a smooth stone. With a flick of her fine-boned wrist, she tossed the rock. It skimmed over the water, bouncing once, twice, six times before it sank below the surface.

"Tell me more about your childhood," he said, and listened as Lou regaled him with stories of her youth. Of when she was sick, and later, of the many unusual lessons her father had taught her.

"No other family?" he asked.

"No." She shaded her eyes. "I had an aunt, but she died when I was a baby. I never knew her at all."

The glowing sun turned her yellow hair white with its beams. "How about you? What about your childhood?" she asked.

He looked out over the water, at the birds dancing in the sky. This just wasn't the time to tell her of his upbringing. He wasn't ready to open himself up to that pain again. He stalled. "We have a lifetime to learn everything."

Her eyes widened with wariness. "Do we?"

"My congregation will approve eventually, Lou. You've done them no wrong."

He watched, perplexed, as her features flashed from joy to uncertainty. He wasn't sure what he had said to cause the change. Reaching for her, he curled her into him in, wrapping his arm around her, loving the feel of her heart beating against his. Pressing on, he sought to soothe her. "I am a man of modest means, a good heart, and a desire to make you the happiest woman under the stars."

Moisture seeped from her eyes into his shirt. "Right here, right now, I am the happiest woman ever. But River Glen . . ."

He tipped up her chin, stopping what he knew was coming next—her worries about being accepted. He lowered his lips, placing them across hers for the briefest of moments. It took all his effort to tear himself from her intoxicating taste. "Do not worry, Lou. From now on, nothing will stand in our way."

Chapter Twelve

The metal rungs creaked as Lou climbed up the steps to the pilothouse. The door had been wedged open with what looked like a knitting needle. A cooling breeze gusted through the doorway and Lou grabbed hold of the railing lest she be pitched into the Mississippi River.

They were departing St. Louis now and Lou would miss it. She'd spent the most glorious two days here with John. He showed her all around the city, but above that, he'd showered her with attention, making her feel special . . . loved. Oh, she hoped it so.

Already, disappointment burned its way through her stomach. The *Amazing Grace* was on its way home. Her time with John was ending. She bit back a sigh and knocked once on the doorframe and stepped in. "Do you have a moment?"

Alex looked up from a bundle of yarn twisted about her fingers that seemed, oddly enough, to knot under her perplexing glare.

"Actually, Lou, I could use an extra pair of hands."

Matt tossed a look over his shoulder, keeping the pilot wheel steady. "Or a sharp pair of shears."

Alex shot him a sour look. To Lou, she said, "Sit, sit." She motioned with a twitch of her jaw to the long expanse of the lazy bench, a long wooden slab running the length of the pilothouse.

Every window in the small room was open wide, yet the heat of the day lingered in the air, causing small droplets of moisture to bead along Lou's hairline. Maybe a fall into the river wouldn't be such a bad thing if it would cool her off.

"What are you making?" In all her years Lou had never seen Alex so much as thread a needle, never mind operate two knitting needles simultaneously.

Alex's brow furrowed as she held up the mass of wool. "You can't tell?"

The bulk of deep-blue yarn looked like a shapeless lump with tentacles. She had no earthly idea what product it could be, but didn't want to hurt Alex's feelings by admitting so.

Lou stared at the back of Matt's head, silently pleading.

"It's a sweater," Alex said brightly. "For Matt. Daphne is teaching me how to knit."

It seemed as though Daphne had become part of the family, and Lou couldn't be happier.

Lou caught Matt's sidelong grimace. She grinned wickedly. "Oh, yes, I see it now." She fingered the thick wool. "He will look utterly dashing in it. All the female passengers will swoon at his feet."

"Oh?" Matt mumbled, a smile hitching the corner of his mouth.

The steamboat rumbled as Matt called, via a set of pipes, down to the boiler room for the engines to slow. He expertly guided the wheel to the left.

"Do you really think so?" Alex stared at the yarn, threading it through her fingers. Her voice shimmered with something Lou couldn't quite identify. Perhaps jealousy? No. Insecurity.

Immediately, Lou felt shame's blush staining her face. Her intent had been to hassle Matt, but it seemed as though Alex was the one her comments affected most. Lou sought to rectify the situation.

"No, I don't think so. If his scowl doesn't frighten the women away, the way he looks at you will make it all too clear that he has eyes for no one but you."

Lou caught the heated look that passed between the two. "Perhaps I should go."

Alex smiled dreamily. "Stay. The pilothouse is a public place."

"Not that it's stopped us before," Matt mumbled.

The red dotting her sister's face mesmerized Lou, but she rose. "I should definitely go."

Reaching out, Alex grabbed Lou's arm. "Sit. Stay. Matthew, apologize for causing Lou discomfort."

Biting back a smile, Lou watched her brother-in-law fumble for words. "Sit," he finally said in the gruff manner Lou had come to love.

"Since you asked so politely." She grinned as she settled herself next to Alex and that infernal blob of yarn.

Alex looped a strand of blue over the needle and sighed in frustration when it didn't catch. "Daphne mentioned you have an admirer in Hank Burnett."

"I don't know if admirer is the right word."

A smile teased her sister's lips. "He brought you fish."

"I know. I think I agreed to go fishing with him."

Alex's hands stilled. "You don't fish. Why would you agree to do such a thing?"

Lou wiped the moisture from her brow. "I don't know. He said he had a cabin and asked if I'd like to go." She turned pleading eyes to her sister. "He's been so kind to me. I just didn't have the heart to say no."

She caught the glance that passed between Matt and Alex. "Enough about Hank and my bad decisions. I didn't come here to talk about him."

"What's on your mind?" Alex asked gently.

Heat crept up Lou's throat and flushed her cheeks. She nibbled on her lip, wondering how she was to pose the questions she yearned to know the answers to.

"Ahh, the reverend."

Inwardly, Lou groaned. "Is it so obvious?"

"Only to someone who's been in your position before— in love."

Alex must have sensed Lou's uncertainty. Using the tip of her finger she nudged up Lou's chin. Lou stared out the window at the passing scenery. Tall reeds swayed in the breeze, and egrets and heron perched lazily on the river-bank. The river was crowded with barges and flats, all vying for space along the river. Soon the boats would peter out, once they were away from the city. She had yet to see another steamer, and was grateful Matt had come up with the ingenious plan of turning the *Amazing Grace* from a freight packet into a glorious hotel.

"What's wrong? I'm fairy sure John returns your feelings. Isn't that a good thing?"

Lou tore her gaze from the gentle waves rolling onto shore. "It's wonderful."

"But?"

Drawing in a deep breath, Lou wondered if she should tell Alex about Madame Angelique. Perhaps then her sister would know how Lou could continue to keep the information from John. For as surely as she was breathing, she knew she'd lose him forever should he find out.

She looked up at Alex, only to find her brown eyes probing. "Or is it River Glen?" Alex rolled the yarn into a massive ball, sweater and all, and stuffed it into a basket.

"Don't let those gossipmongers ruin what you and John have found."

"Amen," Matt growled.

Lou had forgotten he stood but two feet from her. She'd been too wrapped up in her own emotions and he'd been so silent.

"River Glen is but part of the problem."

"What else is there?"

Lou twisted her hands. "Do you and Matt keep secrets from one another? Have you ever?"

"Secrets are a part of any new relationship, Lou, but if a marriage is to work, you must be honest and truthful." Alex's eyebrows dipped. "But you have no secrets from John. He knows all about our upbringing."

Swallowing hard, Lou knew this was the perfect time to ask for Alex's help. Yet she held her tongue. If Madame Angelique's identity were to be revealed, Lou would lose all she'd dreamed. She simply wasn't sure she could perform in front of others without the help of a mask and wig.

"I have no simple advice for you, Lou." Alex picked a piece of blue lint from her coral trousers. "You have to admit that Matthew and I didn't follow the traditional route when we married." Her brown gaze bore into Lou. "Take it one day at a time, one moment. Let the seconds meld into minutes, minutes into days, days into weeks, months. Life has an odd way of working itself out."

What she said made sense. Lou needed to stop fretting about her relationship with John and let it be. But one thing she knew for sure. If she wanted John for a husband, and she truly did, he would have to know about Madame Angelique. She couldn't enter dishonestly into marriage with him.

She would tell him. Perhaps tonight. Certainly before they reached Cincinnati. Losing him forever was a risk she was going to have to take to ensure her happiness.

"Thank you." She kissed her sister's cheek, then side-stepped to kiss Matt's. "Thank you both."

Matt smiled. "Stay out of trouble."

Lou gave her best impression of innocence. "Don't I always?"

They both stared at her, and in tandem said, "No."

Dusk settled as the sun crept toward the horizon. John tore off a chunk of bread he'd hoarded from lunch and tossed it toward the birds on the riverbank.

One day. That was all the time he had left alone with Lou. The past thirteen days had been amazing. Lou was amazing. Ever since they'd left St. Louis, she had been by his side—except for late at night, after dinner, when she went off to help Jack in the Gaming Hall. The way Lou loved her family only added to the feelings he held for her. His congregation had to accept her, because he feared he'd never be able to let her go.

He heard a creak behind him and a stole a glance over his shoulder. No one was there. For days now he'd sensed someone following him. Ever since he and Lou had heard rustling at the river days ago he'd been more aware.

Even in St. Louis when they'd docked for two days, he'd heard footsteps behind him when no one lurked, the rustle of clothes when he was alone. It made no sense.

Like now.

He peeked again over his shoulder as he tossed another piece of bread into the darkening night. He appeared to be alone, yet instinct told him he wasn't.

Could it be Hank? He hoped so. It was time they'd had it out with each other, once and for all. With more force than necessary, he heaved the remainder of the bread towards shore. Along with the squawking of the birds, his heart pounded.

He'd had enough.

Seeking an open spot into which he could finally lure his stalker, John inched his way down the railing. At the far end of the boat, planks opened wide into a small gathering area. He ducked around the corner and waited, holding his breath.

Finally, soft footsteps fell on the wooden deck. John jumped out. A shrill scream rent the air as a woman grabbed her heart.

"Grandmother?!"

Shock had John back stepping in retreat. It couldn't be.

Eloisa Scranton Regent gasped for breath. "You scared the dickens out of me, John Scranton Hewitt!"

Reaching out, he touched her, just to be sure she was real and not a figment of his imagination. Oftentimes when he was younger, before she had come to live with his father and him, he'd often conjured her image to ease the loneliness.

She patted his hand as his mouth dropped open. "Surprised?"

"Yes. No. Yes." His head swam. He thought he'd seen her a few times: in the town near the river, in St. Louis, and aboard during Madame Angelique's performances, but had dismissed the notion as impossible. She was supposed to be in New York.

He grabbed her hands and squeezed them. "What are you doing here?"

"When you weren't home, I found out where you were."

"Home?"

"In River Glen," she said as if he were thick in the head.

"But how?"

"When your housekeeper told me of your trip, I decided to board also, though it wasn't easy at the last minute."

A light mist began to fall. "You've been aboard for nearly two weeks?"

Her eyes darted to the side. "Er, yes." As the mist turned to rain, she tugged him toward the double doors leading inside. They passed the Gaming Hall, which was silent this time of day.

"Have you been following me for all that time?"

Her guilty blush gave him his answer. He shoved a hand through his hair, opened his mouth, and snapped it closed again. He didn't know which question to ask first.

"I've spent many days hiding behind fans and potted plants, not to mention other passengers, to keep you from spotting me. It hasn't been easy, dear."

All he could do was gape.

"I know this is a shock. . . ."

Shock? That was stating it mildly. "What," John asked, "were you doing in Cincinnati in the first place?"

Surprise tugged at the lines around her mouth. "Didn't you get my letter?"

He would have laughed if he hadn't been so stunned that she was standing before him. Her travel plans must have been in the letter that had been caught in the rain. "I did receive a letter from you, but it was inadvertently destroyed."

She steered him toward the boat's library. "So you don't know?"

"Know what?" As they settled themselves into large wingback chairs, he took a moment to look at her. It had been years since he saw her last. Remembering the last day he'd spent with her, he winced.

"I have terrible news for you, John."

The look on her face worried him. "What?"

"Your father . . ." She plucked at the fabric on her ornately embroidered shirtwaist. "He passed away a month ago." Her gaze, as blue as his own and as blue as his mother's had been, swept over his face. "The news was also in the letter I wrote."

John leaned back into the chair and dropped his head into his hands. His father was gone. Part of John had always hoped they would reconcile. Now that hope drifted away as if swept up in the wake of the steamboat.

"I'm sorry, John."

"I am too, though I suppose we said all we had to say to each other."

"Is that so?"

His head shot up at the sarcasm in her tone. "You know it is."

"I know there was much said, but I do not believe for a moment that you said all you had to say, or that your stubborn father told you all you needed to hear."

Old emotions, ones John thought long buried, surfaced, "And what is it you think I needed to hear?"

Her large bangle bracelets jangled as she clasped her hands together. "Why, that you were loved above and beyond all else."

He turned away from her, from her eyes that reminded him so much of his mother's and stared out the large, curved library windows. On the banks of the river, children frolicked in the rain and waved at the *Amazing Grace* as it floated by. He focused on the children as they played, and still stared long after they had disappeared from view. Anything to keep his emotions at bay.

"You were, John. Loved above all else."

He turned back to her. Light spilled across his grandmother's face, highlighting the thick lines that creased her eyes, her lips.

"You didn't always know it," she said, "but it was there, whether the words were said or not."

Laughter floated through the open door as people walked down the hall. Laughing was the last thing he felt like doing. "I find that hard to believe."

The corner of her lip quirked. "That's because you're as stubborn as he was."

He drew his right leg on top his left knee. "I'm nothing like he was."

She laughed, but there was nothing humorous about the sound. "You're more like him that you care to admit."

Heat beat against his cheeks. "How so?"

She spoke with her hands, turning palms up as she explained. "You're both runners."

It was manners, pure and simple, that kept him from calling her delusional. The muscle in his jaw ached with the effort to remain silent.

She ran her hand over a stack of books on the table separating their chairs. She picked one up, glanced at the first page, then set it down again. "Your father ran from his emotions. You run from confrontation."

If he hadn't been trying to devise ways to excuse himself, he'd have argued her point. "Go on."

"You run, John."

"I didn't run when Father stood in front of five hundred friends and denounced my decision to attend the seminary."

"No, you waited until you returned home. You packed up without saying so much as a good-bye." Tears swam in her blue eyes. "What your father believed, or what he'd like to have others believe, were not necessarily the opinions of all." She sniffed and reached for a handkerchief tucked into her sleeve. "You are all the blood family I have left, John, and you walked out on me."

Guilt crashed into him. He was a man of God, one who was supposed to set an example for others. Yet he'd been selfish and cruel.

"I'm so sorry," he said.

"I know what your father did hurt you terribly, but I think he suffered more. His intentions were never to force you to leave, but rather to have you rethink your career.

How badly he wanted you, his only child, to become his business partner. He became a shadow of a man after you left."

"Why didn't he write?"

"Pride. Stubbornness. I think he thought you'd turn him away, as he'd done to you."

"I wouldn't have."

"I know, and I tried to tell him, but he wouldn't listen."

As all she told him sank in, remorse and regret slammed into him. Years wasted in anger, in hurt. For both him and his father.

Sorrow permeated his words. "It's too late now."

"Is it?" his grandmother asked.

"He's dead. No amends can be made."

Tipping her head to the side, she pursed her lips. "What if I lied?"

Emotions swept through him, jumbling together, and he couldn't figure out *what* to feel. "About what?"

"Your father. He's fit as a fiddle."

John jumped to his feet. Shock rippled through him. "He's alive? Why would you lie about something like death?"

Eloisa stayed sitting. Her keen eyes narrowed. "Would you have listened to me, John? Heard all I had to say? Heard it in your heart?"

Swallowing hard, he shook his head. He would have been stubborn and childish.

"I knew I needed to do something drastic to reunite the two of you. Go to him, John. He loves you, and you love him. Let him see the man you've become, and let him show you that he can be the father you always wanted."

He pushed the heel of his hand into his eye. "I don't know. I need time to think."

Eloisa rose to her feet. "I understand."

After a long moment of staring blankly out the rain-splattered window, John crossed over to her and took her hands in his own. "Either way," he said, "I'm glad you're here. I've missed you."

"And I you. So very much." Looping her arm through his, she said, "Tell me about this River Glen. I want to hear all about your new life."

"I'll tell you all about it over dinner. You don't have plans, do you? There's someone I'd like to introduce you to."

"That lovely LouEllen? We've met, but I'd love to join you both."

His mouth dropped open. "How did you—" He smiled. "I'd forgotten you've been following me. I hope you didn't get poison ivy the day you hid in the bushes by the river."

Her head tipped. "The river?"

"Yes. The day we stopped in Canoe Falls."

"It wasn't me. After you nearly spotted me on the street, I headed back to the boat."

He led her down a flight of stairs toward the dining room. "Why *were* you following me? Why not just seek me out the first day we boarded the boat?"

She paused, drawing him to a stop. "I rather wanted to see the kind of man you had become. For I'm sure if it wasn't for my influence in your young life, you would have been more sinner than saint."

"I'm no saint."

"Oh, I know that quite well." She grinned. "Beyond that, I wasn't sure how I'd be received. You never answered a single one of my letters . . ."

He was a fool for turning his back on those who loved him, but could he return? Wounded pride had him thinking no, but his heart ached for parental love and acceptance.

He squeezed his grandmother's hand as they stepped into the dining room. She'd been deceitful and manipulative, and he'd never been more grateful.

Lou's words echoed through his head. *Besides, sometimes lying is for the best and shouldn't be considered a sin at all.*

Who would have thought a reverend would believe such a statement true? Yet he did. He couldn't even stay angry with Eloisa for following him for two weeks. If he had known she was aboard, he would not have given Lou his undivided attention.

Where was Lou?

His grandmother smiled from across the table and a sudden uneasiness took hold of him.

If not his grandmother, who had been spying in the bushes?

Chapter Thirteen

Lou checked the clock for the fifth time in five minutes. Where was Daphne? She'd sent her to find John an hour ago, to tell him she couldn't make it to dinner that night.

This would be Madame Angelique's last show. The *Amazing Grace* was due to dock in Cincinnati tomorrow. She had spent all afternoon preparing and rehearsing, not just for her last performance, but also for the conversation she needed to have with John.

The minute hand swept slowly toward the 12. Ten more minutes until she was due on stage. Or rather, Madame Angelique was due on stage.

In her mind she'd gone over and over how she'd tell John her secret, what she'd say. Her whole future relied on his reaction, and it was her words that would seal her fate.

Would he forgive her her lies? Would he condemn her? Would he insist she give up performing as Madame Angelique? Could she give up her dream of singing for the love of a man? Absolutely, she would, if that was what he wished.

Her footsteps echoed as she crept through the backstage door and peeked through the curtain. The Gentlemen's

Lounge was crowded with both men and women. Her debut show nearly two weeks ago had put an end to the male-only regulations. As word of mouth spread of Madame Angelique's talent, more and more women began accompanying their spouses to the show.

More than once Lou had seen Mrs. Scranton Regent lurking in the back corners of the room. John had seen every show as far as she knew. Perhaps since he enjoyed Madame Angelique he'd be more accepting of the person who lurked behind the mask?

She could only hope.

The minute hand pulsed forward. It wasn't like Daphne to be late. What was keeping her?

Sitting at the small vanity table, Lou stared at the cosmetics. Rouge for her cheeks, that much Lou knew, but what blend of colors to use on her eyes? With a few swipes of cotton Daphne made her look exotic and alluring. At her own hand, Lou feared she's look like a clown from the traveling circus.

Without Daphne's help, Lou never would have been able to transform. It had been Daphne's idea to use several masks, not just one, and to add height with shoe wedges. Also, it had been her idea to add cleavage in the way of cotton wadding. No one could possibly associate the tall, alluring, curvaceous Madame Angelique with Lou.

Lou didn't need to check the clock to know several minutes had passed. There was no use for it. She'd have to try her hand with the cosmetics and hope for the best.

Ten minutes later, and five minutes past her curtain time, Lou had been transformed. After a week, she'd finally managed not to wobble on the shoes with the five-inch wedges, but she still had trouble adjusting her wig by herself.

A quick look in the mirror revealed that she'd have to put a sniffle into her routine because Madame Angelique looked decidedly ill.

With a deep fortifying breath, she heaved her faux bosoms and headed for the door that led to the stage.

If this were to be the last performance of her lifetime, she was going to enjoy every note. Yet she couldn't ignore the dread and worry that lined her stomach, and it had nothing to do with her upcoming conversation with John.

What had become of Daphne?

John checked his pocket watch, noting that Madame Angelique was running behind schedule. From wall to wall people crowded the room, waiting for the show to begin.

His shoulders stiff with tension, he leaned back in his seat, then forward. He shifted one leg atop the other, then reversed the order.

He wondered what had happened to Lou. When he had inquired, no one had seen her since lunch.

"Do stop fidgeting, John."

He glanced at his grandmother, still unable to believe she was really here, that she really cared.

It festered inside him, what she had said. Did he run away from his problems, his fears, instead of facing them head-on? It was true he'd left home without a backward glance. He thought everyone had felt the same and hadn't thought twice about giving up all he'd ever known.

Yet according to Eloisa, he'd had allies all along, and had ignored them in favor of his self-righteous stubbornness.

Had his father really changed? Could John find the courage to go back and face his greatest fear: being rejected yet again?

"You're still fidgeting."

He planted his feet firmly on the floor. "Sorry," he mumbled.

"Is it LouEllen that has you so restless? I'm sure she's fine."

"You're probably right."

"Was tonight the night you were planning to propose?"

His mouth dropped open. Tonight had been the night he was going to ask for Lou's hand. He'd found a ring in St. Louis, a small amethyst the color of her eyes. He wondered exactly how much his grandmother had witnessed between him and Lou.

He was saved from answering her queries when the gaslights dimmed and the curtains parted.

With a flurry of feathers, Madame Angelique glided across the stage, a song already floating from her lips.

John closed his eyes, as he always did when listening to her sing, and let her voice wash over him. What was it about her songs that mesmerized him so?

Behind him, he heard the creak of the door as it opened and swooshed closed.

He jumped as a hand settled on his shoulder. Turning, he found Jack staring at him with wide, frightened blue eyes. "Can you come with me, Reverend?"

John was on his feet before Jack could finish the question. His pulse thrummed as fear coursed through his body. "What's happened?" he asked as soon as they reached the empty hallway.

"It's—" Jack pulled in a shuddering breath. "It's Daphne."

She tugged on his hand, leading him down a series of passageways, and finally up the stairs toward the crew's quarters.

Jack paused outside a door with the brass number 7 dangling crookedly on its paneling. She knocked once and entered. John followed and stopped dead in his tracks. A second later, he was pushed into the room from behind. Spinning, he found his grandmother behind him.

"Dear Lord," she said.

He silently finished the prayer as Eloisa rushed to the bed. "You poor child," she crooned.

Lou's dear friend Daphne lay still, her eyes closed, her breathing labored. Her lip was split and swollen, and a small bruise was forming near her eye, just below a cut on her forehead.

Matt and Jack stood sentry next to the bed, their faces awash in dismay.

Alex perched on the edge of the down mattress, stone still, as though she feared coming too close.

Eloisa unbuttoned her cuffs and rolled up her sleeves. "Wash pan?" she asked.

"I'll get it." Jack ran for the door, the fringe on her leather boots flying in her wake.

John knelt bedside and took hold of Daphne's cold hands. "What happened to her?"

Matt shifted. "Jack decided to retire early. She was coming back to her room when she heard muffled moans. She called out, but no one answered. When she reached the hallway, she found Daphne slumped by the door."

John nodded to Daphne. "Has she spoken?"

Jack came in carrying a washbasin, the water splashing over the rim. "No, she hasn't awoken since I found her. I think she hit her head on the hall table as she fell."

Eloisa dipped a cloth into the water and wrung it out. "This gash here will need stitching. I can do it, but it's been years."

Alex rose. "Lou's rather good at it. I'll go find her."

"Lou," Daphne murmured.

Alex patted Daphne's hand. "I'll find her. Don't worry. Everything will be okay," she said. She started toward the door. "Has anyone seen Lou?" Her dark gaze shot to John.

"Last I saw her was at lunch. She mentioned to me that she needed to help Jack again tonight."

Jack's head shot up. "Again?"

Confusion clouded his mind. "Yes. In the Gaming Hall? She's been helping you every night."

"There must be some mistake."

"This certainly isn't the time to hash it out," Alex said, her hand on the doorknob. "I'll see if I can find her and discreetly ask if there are any doctors aboard."

As John kept hold of Daphne's hands, praying silently for her, his mind slipped to Lou several times. If she hadn't been with Jack, then where? Was it possible she'd been with Hank?

Hank!

John looked down at Daphne. Was it possible? Certainly it was. He looked at Matt and nodded toward the door. Eloisa continued to wash and soothe, comforting not only Daphne, but also all those present.

Matt met him in the hall. John cleared his throat, anger burning inside. Rubbing his hands across his forehead, he said in a low tone, "I might know who—"

He broke off and leaned on the wall, banging his head against the plaster. This was his fault. If he had warned the Parkers, Hank wouldn't have been aboard. Daphne's assault weighed on his shoulders, boring into his guilty conscience.

Matt straightened and pushed his hand through his hair. "Who, Reverend?"

A low moan escaped John's lips. Rage and frustration sat heavy in his stomach. He'd taken vows to protect others, yet by protecting the sins of one, he'd failed an innocent person. And still he couldn't bring himself to release the information.

"I can't," he said in a ragged sigh.

Grabbing John's shoulders, Matt shook him. "What do you mean you ca—" He broke off and let John go. "Your collar?"

John nodded. Moisture dripped from the back of his neck down his shirt. He forced himself to release his clenched fists, but a second later they were once again curled in anger.

"Damn all to hell!" Matt said through tight lips.

John was inclined to agree. He pulled back his shoulders, knowing he had to do something. His skin vibrated with the hatred he held inside. "I can't say the words, Matt, but who am I to stop you from guessing?"

Matt's steel-gray eyes glinted with fury. "Guess?"

"Yes."

Matt closed his eyes. "A man, obviously. Someone you and I both know?"

John nodded.

"This can take forever!"

Softly, John said, "I heard his sins, Matt."

Matt's eyes widened. "Someone from River Glen!" His eyes narrowed as the information registered. "Hank Burnett."

Relief that the truth was out at last, John slumped against the wall. After a moment, he felt Matt's hand settle on his shoulder.

"I don't envy you your job, Reverend. Keeping something like that to myself would eat me up inside, but you already know what that's about, don't you?" Without waiting for a response, he said, "I'll gather up my men and search the boat. We'll find him."

John watched as Matt hurried down the hallway, murder in his eyes. John feared his eyes mirrored the same emotion.

He glanced up at the sound of rapid footsteps. Alex turned the corner and nearly barreled into him.

Worry tinged her eyes, her voice. "I can't find Lou!" Her knuckles had gone white from being squeezed so tightly. "You don't think . . . She couldn't be another victim, could she?"

John surged to his feet. He hadn't even thought of the possibility, but it made sense. Lou was the one Hank wanted.

"Where have you looked?" John asked, trying to keep his tone calm.

The door swung open and Eloisa stepped out, her face pale. "Daphne's more conscious now. She's going to be just fine." Wringing her hands, Eloisa said, her voice hushed, "Daphne said that a man named Hank Burnett was the one who hurt her. Said he was looking for Lou, and when Daphne wouldn't tell him where she was, he turned violent. Thank heavens Jack showed up when she did."

The relief John felt at hearing of Daphne's improvement was completely overshadowed by his fear. "I've got to find Lou."

Eloisa's hand settled on his arm. "Daphne also mentioned that Madame Angelique would know where to find Lou."

"Her show is just ending," Alex said.

"I'll go." He had to do something or he'd hunt down Hank and kill him himself.

Alex nodded and looked more than a bit ashen as John rushed for the stairs. He was so taken aback by the night's events that he completely forgot to knock on the dressing room door before he pushed it open.

Madame Angelique had her back to him, a coppery-colored wig in one hand, a mask in the other. Golden hair flowed down her back and shone under the dim lighting.

It hit him hard, and even harder still when she turned in surprise, a guilty blush tipping her ears.

His voice cracked. "Lou?"

Chapter Fourteen

"**I**'m so sorry I've been keeping it from you. I was going to tell you tonight," she said with a gentle shrug of her shoulders.

Lou was Madame Angelique. He stared openly at the color on her eyelids, the rouge sweeping up her cheeks. Staggering back, he could do nothing but gape. "Why?" he finally managed to say through a throat clogged with shock and confusion.

"Because you needed to know. I couldn't continue to lie to you, to keep this secret. I—" Her breath hitched.

He interrupted. "No, why keep this—" he gestured to her cosmetics, her mask, her wig, her . . . her breasts. He averted his gaze quickly. "Why a secret? Why not just go out there as yourself?"

She crossed to a small table and removed the cover of a small jar. Dipping her hands inside, she slathered a creamy substance on her face and wiped it with a white cloth. When she turned back to him, her skin was devoid of all color, looking pale and ghost-like in the dim light of the small dressing room.

Tears had gathered in her eyes. "I was such a pathetic child," she murmured.

"Lou—"

She held up her hand. "No, please. Let me finish. I've never told anyone of this, and the words . . . they do not come easy, so please."

What could he say? That she would trust him with something kept long buried in her soul made him feel honored, yet another part of him didn't want to hear the words, to see her pain, because he knew he'd feel the hurt she harbored as much as she did.

"I was so different from my sisters, and I felt isolated and lonely. Since I was often sick, I couldn't participate in the things they did to gain my father's approval. So I sought to find my own way to win him over. When I was seven, I constructed a small stage and practiced songs for weeks in advance. Music had been my salvation during those years, and I loved it with a passion that had no equal."

Her gaze drifted to him as she spoke those last few words. In her eyes he saw what she felt for him, and it humbled him that he had earned her love. He sensed where her story was headed, and his heart broke for her. Though he longed to go to her—to take her in his arms, to pacify her inner demons—he stayed where he was, listening. He had to wonder when the last time anyone before him had taken the time to just listen to Lou, to hear what she had to say.

Softly, he asked, "What happened?"

She looked up at him, a small smile tweaking her lips, but her eyes remained far away. Her chin nudged into the air. "I sang for my father . . . and he hated it."

He winced. "Surely he didn't say such a thing?"

She bent down and untied an impossibly high shoe. "He didn't have to. He said nothing; his silence spoke loud enough." She tossed the shoe aside and went to work on its mate. "Whenever I tried to sing in front of people after that, I froze. Words would not come through my lips, only a strangled whine. All I could see in my mind was my father's face, devoid of any emotion, staring at me as though he couldn't believe I was his child."

John knelt down beside her and looked up into her angelic face. Using the pad of his thumb, he traced her cheekbone. She amazed him. Frightened to sing in front of others, she had resorted to donning a costume to fulfill her dream when others might have just let the dreams die and the resentment grow.

"I never knew your father personally, Lou, but I have to believe he never meant to hurt you. Surely you know that?"

A tear crept from her eye and rolled down her cheek. "I know he loved me because I was his child. But I always felt as though he never loved me for who I was. He never really knew me at all. No one, besides you, really does. No one has ever taken the time."

He gentled his words, hoping they didn't sound harsh. He pressed his finger to the lone tear, absorbing the moisture. "Has no one taken the time, Lou? Or have you not allowed the real you to be known?"

Her gaze locked with his. Silence reigned over the room. She cupped his face with her small hand, brushing her thumb over his cheek.

"I think, Lou, it's time to be honest, not only with each other, but with ourselves."

She slipped out of the chair and into his lap. Wrapping her arms around his neck, she let her head rest on his shoulder. Moisture from her eyes seeped into his shirt. He held her tight, his stomach in knots.

"I should probably tell you," she said into his shirt, "that before I met you I was content to live a lie. To tell lies to others to make them see me the way I wanted to be seen." She lifted her head and looked at him. "But with you . . . I wanted you to know me. All of me, not just the person everyone else saw." She swallowed hard. "Yet even before you saw my temper, witnessed my manipulations firsthand, I felt you knew me. Really knew me. And cared for me nonetheless."

He slid his fingers through her hair. "There is nothing about you not to care for, or not to love. You must know by now that I love you, Lou. I love your temper, your zest for life. I love that you know how to swing a baseball bat, and I even love that you can't cook, but still you try."

She sniffled, and red blotches began to dot her face as tears flowed freely from her eyes. The words were a whisper from her lips. "I love you too."

She used her feather stole to wipe her tears. "You're not angry with me?"

"For what?"

"For being Madame Angelique?"

"I'm nothing but proud of you, Lou. For reaching for a dream and achieving it any way you had to do it."

"But what of your congregation?"

He stiffened. His congregation all thought of Madame Angelique as a fallen woman. How on earth was he to convince them otherwise?

His grandmother's words echoed. *Your father ran from his emotions. You run from confrontation.* This time he wouldn't run. This time he'd fight for what he wanted. His congregation would just have to understand, or he didn't want to guide that particular flock anymore if they couldn't see the love he had for this woman and accept it—unconditionally.

She wriggled in his grasp, and he saw the devastation in her eyes. She obviously thought his silence meant he'd chosen his congregation over her.

Pushing him away, she jumped to her feet and headed to the door.

"Lou, wait!"

The door opened before Lou could turn the knob, and a head peeked in. "LouEllen, is that you?"

"Grandmother?" John said.

Lou's jaw dropped. "Grandmother?" She turned accusing eyes on John. "Eloisa Scranton Regent of the New York Regents is your grandmother? You're—you're rich?"

Thankfully, his grandmother blocked the doorway so Lou couldn't escape. "I can explain. Please give me a minute."

Lou's nub of a chin shot into the air. Her violet eyes blazed fire. Red splotches dotted her fair skin, marring her creamy complexion. "Mrs. Scranton Regent, would you please excuse me?" The words seemed to be strangled through Lou's lips rather than spoken.

Eloisa gaped at John. "You haven't told her about Daphne?"

John scraped a hand over his face. "I haven't had the chance." He felt bad for forgetting about the girl altogether.

Lou grabbed Eloisa's arm. "Daphne? Is she all right?"

"No, my dear." Eloisa settled her fingers over Lou's shaking hand. "She's been attacked."

A gasp rent the air, and Lou's eyes went wide. With a hand over her mouth, she brushed past Eloisa and disappeared out the door.

"You can't avoid him forever, Lou." Jack helped Daphne spoon a bit of broth into her swollen mouth. "You rip up his notes without even reading them, you throw his flowers overboard, and give the candy he buys to the children on the Landing."

In her head, a small hammer pounded Lou's temples. She'd had a headache for days. Running a brush through Daphne's hair, she did her best to cheer her good friend.

"You're looking better every hour. All that swelling will be gone soon, and you'll be as good as new."

She choked back tears. That Daphne had kept her secret under such duress humbled her. She'd never had such a dear friend.

The silver spoon clinked against the porcelain bowl. "Ignoring me will not make me go away," Jack said.

Oh, but Lord, she wished it would. For days now she'd had to listen to everyone from Matt to Doc, the cook, extol John's virtues.

"Are you just going to let him go?"

"He already left."

Once they reached Cincinnati, John didn't even try to see her one last time before he left the boat. Didn't that prove something?

"He had no choice, Lou. He had a sermon to give." Jack jabbed a finger in the air. "And you weren't doing anything to keep him here, on board. How many times did he reach out, only to have his efforts scoffed at?"

Something tightened in Lou's chest. They hadn't been there when he made the decision to choose his congregation over her. They hadn't felt him stiffen, or seen the look in his eyes when faced with the knowledge that he'd need to tell his congregation she was Madame Angelique.

She fought to erase the image of his horrified features as he stiffened with the realization that his congregation would learn of her identity.

He'd chosen them over her and that was all there was to it. No amount of sappy letters, flowers, or chocolate would change that fact.

He simply didn't love her enough. And she loved him too much to settle for less.

Daphne peered at her, the skin surrounding her left eye a myriad of colors ranging from the lightest yellows to the deepest purples. Lou still couldn't believe Hank had been behind the brutal attack. Yet Daphne had always been ill at ease when Hank was around. What had she been able to see that Lou hadn't?

Daphne said to Jack, "You forgot to mention that she cries herself to sleep every night."

Jack nodded. "You're right. I did forget to mention how you cry yourself to sleep at night."

Daphne shook her head. Her gaze landed on Lou. "Those blotches are doing terrible things to your skin."

Lou jumped to her feet, her hands fisted at her sides. To Jack, she said, "Did I remind you all the days you moped around when Cal left? Did I? Do I mention to you how you drive everyone crazy when the mail boat floats by? Do I?" she asked, her voice rising, and not even caring that Jack had paled at her words.

Jack set the bowl on the table and rose, facing Lou across the bed. "Yes, I mope. Yes, I cannot wait to hear from Cal. You can be assured, Lou Parker, that when Cal takes the time to write me a letter," she shouted, "that I don't tear it into tiny pieces!"

Lou set her hands on her hips. "Which is just about the saddest thing I've ever seen, considering you two don't even like each other. Or . . . so . . . you . . . say!"

Jack's nostrils flared. "I think I liked you better when you were quiet and had no opinions."

"Well, get used to the new me because I'm not changing back." She headed for the door. "Daphne looks like she needs a drink of lemonade."

Daphne sputtered, and Lou rushed to reassure. "Don't worry, I won't make it."

She opened the door and bumped right into Mrs. Scranton Regent. "Oh!"

"Hello, my dear."

"I thought you had gone back to New York."

"I decided I couldn't leave until matters were settled." She held out a gloved hand. "May I have a word?"

Lou's head dropped. She'd avoided the older woman those last days of the *Amazing Grace*'s journey and was now ashamed. Eloisa had been nothing but kind to her. "Come with me to the kitchen?" Lou asked.

"Certainly."

They walked in silence for a moment before Eloisa said, "Any news on Daphne's attacker?"

Lou shook her head. "No." Matt had searched the boat top to bottom that night with no luck, until one of the passengers spotted Hank swimming downriver. Before anyone could jump in, he'd swum ashore. The area had been searched, but Hank had disappeared. She sighed. "The law is looking for him—not only along river towns, but also here in Cincinnati, should he be foolish enough to return."

The carpeted stairs muffled their footsteps as they stepped onto the Texas Deck's landing and headed for the stairs leading into the galley.

Turning toward the older woman, Lou said, "I have a feeling you didn't come to speak to me about Hank."

"No. I wish to speak to you about John."

Lou sighed. "I wish you wouldn't. I have nothing to say."

"He loves you, LouEllen."

Tears smarted her eyes. "Not enough."

The older woman took hold of Lou's hand. "I will not fight John's battles for him, but there are things you need to know. Things he should have, and would have, I am quite sure, told you."

The implication was clear. Eloise was trying to gently point out that Lou had left without giving John a chance to explain.

Despite herself, the stirrings of curiosity took hold. "What sort of things?"

Mrs. Scranton Regent guided her down the hall. "Things that will, perhaps, help you understand just a little bit better. Then you can judge for yourself if he deserves your forgiveness."

Chapter Fifteen

Her feet dangling over the end of the bed, Lou sat in the dark.

Could she go to John after all the misery she'd put him through? Ask his forgiveness? Offer hers?

Eloisa had explained John's upbringing in high society New York—every heartbreaking, rigid detail. Her heart ached at the shame and humiliation he must have felt when his father denounced his only son for not becoming his exact replica. And broke yet again when Eloisa explained how John's father longed for John's forgiveness.

So similar, their backgrounds, yet so different in the way each had dealt with the blow of their fathers' rejection. She had shrunken into herself, never allowing her true character to be known, whereas John had left New York and his family . . . and his money. He'd never looked back, staying true to himself and his beliefs.

His actions all made sense, now that she could see them clearly. All thanks to Eloisa. Lou pulled a thread on her duvet and watched as the hem unraveled. The boat rocked a gentle lullaby as she tormented herself over things she should have done or said.

She'd thought he'd rejected her by choosing his congregation over her, an echo of her painful childhood memories. However, after the acceptance John had shown her, she should have stayed and listened to his explanation. Instead, she'd allowed her foolish stubbornness to rule her behavior.

Lou scooted back under the covers as she heard a key in the lock.

Jack pushed open the door, a shaft of light from the hallway chasing her into the room. She caught sight of Lou and sighed. "You haven't gone to him yet?"

Was it so pitifully obvious by the look on her face? The door clicked as it closed and the room plunged into darkness.

"I don't know if I can. I've been such a fool."

The rattle of glass resonated just before Jack lit a match. She replaced the cover to the gaslight before turning back to Lou.

"You can."

A soft glow from the light thrust the room into long, irregular shadows.

"I'm not sure. I need to think."

"A good night's sleep will help." She turned down the cover on her bed and opened the small window above her headboard.

Lou shifted. "I want to apologize for my outburst earlier."

Jack sat on her bed and took off her boots. "Already forgotten."

"I'm glad to hear of Cal's return." She noted her sister's hesitant expression. "I thought you'd be happier."

Tossing the other boot on the floor with its mate, Jack looked up, her vivid blue eyes pained. "What of this Charlotte he's bringing with him? Do you think—" She shook her head, her dark hair cascading over her shoulders.

Lou also had some questions about this mysterious

woman who was returning to the *Amazing Grace* with Cal. Who was she, and exactly how did Cal know her? "I'm sure he'll explain everything once he arrives next month."

"I hope you're right." Jack slipped into her worn nightdress. Once settled in bed, she fluffed the pillow before resting her head. "May I ask you something that has been bothering me?"

Lou had been waiting for the probing questions regarding Madame Angelique's identity, but as of yet, her family had been supportive, if not a bit surprised.

"Certainly. I can't guarantee I will answer it, however."

Jack tossed a pillow at her. "John mentioned something to me the other day, before we docked—"

Bolting upright, Lou said, "You spoke to him? What did he say?"

"I'd tell you if you allowed me to finish."

Clamping her lips closed Lou leaned back.

"He mentioned your memories of Father."

Pressing the thin sheet around her, Lou considered how to respond. Once, she would have rushed to change the subject, but now . . . She had changed. She no longer wanted to act the role of Lou Parker—she wanted to *be* Lou Parker.

"What of them?"

"Aunt Marilee was a singer, did you know?"

Her father's sister? Her father had spoken of Aunt Marilee infrequently and had never mentioned her lifestyle. "No, I didn't."

"He didn't want that kind of life for you, Lou. If he showed any disdain toward your singing, it was only because it brought back painful memories of his sister."

Aunt Marilee had died when Lou was a baby; of the fever, she recalled her mother saying.

"You're quite like her, you know. Your hair, your coloring, your voice."

Shock rolled over Lou. Her father must have been stunned, seeing her that day she performed for him. No wonder he looked as though he'd seen a ghost.

"He was scared, Lou."

Scared? "Of what?"

"Of losing you too. Not only to a world he knew nothing about, but to a life that runs you ragged, until there's nothing left but an empty shell. No energy or will to fight off illness. Aunt Marilee spent her time traveling from one city to the next to perform, no stops, no vacations. Life was always about the next job."

"Oh." If he had only told her about her aunt . . . "Why didn't he tell me?"

"I think he felt you, at seven, were too young to know all the details. That he'd tell you when you were older. But then you stopped singing, and the matter was dropped completely."

Her eyes narrowed. "How did you know?"

"Alex. She remembers Aunt Marilee quite well."

Alex would have been five when Aunt Marilee died. "Why didn't anyone tell me?" All the years she spent thinking her father disfavored her . . . when it had been grief that sent him running from the room, not her.

Jack shrugged. "I always thought Mother had told you."

Lou shook her head. Slowly, the information Jack shared sank in. All these years she had felt as though her father had abandoned her emotionally, and now to find out he hadn't . . .

"What's wrong?" Jack asked. "I would have thought this would clarify things for you. Father loved you, Lou. Whether you sang or not. Don't you remember the way he looked at you? At all of us?"

Tears clouded her eyes. She did remember. Oh, she had been so blind to have not seen it before! Moisture seeped from her eyes. She'd been so foolish. Self-centered and foolish! She'd kept in her pain instead of sharing it. If only she'd gone to her father, had asked . . .

"I never did understand why you stopped singing, but now I do. I wish I had known then so you wouldn't have been in silent pain all these years."

"But what—" Lou cleared her throat. "What would Father think of me now? Now that I've realized his fears?"

Jack's voice held a hint of censure. "He'd be proud, Lou. Of all you've accomplished. You've retained everything he taught you, yet you were strong enough to seek something you believed in. You're not like Marilee, consumed with performance. You're *you*."

For years she'd thought her father had rejected her, when in truth she'd been the one holding back. And with a start, she realized she was repeating her mistake with John.

She needed to find him, and if that meant swallowing her pride and seeking him out, she would.

Come first light, she'd go to him.

She thought again of her father, seeing him now in a different light than the one her young eyes had seen him through. A warm glow spread over her, knowing he had loved her, yet at the same time a sense of sadness remained. She'd denied her father the chance to know her because of her mulish beliefs. She'd lost so much time with him. Silently, she promised she'd make him proud of her now.

Rolling onto her side, she asked, "How's Daphne?"

"Resting. She's very lucky."

Which was something all of them had known from the beginning, especially after what they had learned of Hank's past.

Lou shuddered, remembering the way he had looked at her, the way he had touched her. How had he fooled everybody so easily? "Do you think they'll find him?" she asked.

"I do. Sooner or later he's going to make a mistake, Lou. It's just a matter of time."

How much time? she wondered. Did he see her choosing of John as a rejection of him? Would he come after her? Even thought Matt had guards posted along the boat's stage and decks, how safe were they?

She pushed the matter out of her head. If she dwelled on the possibilities, she'd have nightmares.

"Don't worry," Jack said. "You'll not make the same mistake Alex did months ago and venture out alone, will you?"

Back in New Orleans, if Matt hadn't found Alex in time, her sister would be gone. No, Lou wouldn't make the same error. She'd take every caution to ensure her safety, and pray Hank was caught soon.

"I prom—"

A gentle knocking interrupted her. Jack sighed and pushed her covers aside. At the door she called out, "Who is it?"

"Alex."

Jack turned the lock and opened the door. Alex peeked her head into the room. "Something just arrived for you, Lou."

"What?"

Alex came into the room carrying a wooden birdcage. A small canary rested on a perch inside.

Jack's eyes widened. "He sent you a bird?"

Alex's eyes glowed with amusement. "I think it's terribly romantic." She set the cage on the bed.

Jack moaned. "You would. It smells worse than a stable," she said, wrinkling her nose.

"Only because you, for some incomprehensible reason, like the smell of a stable," Alex countered.

Lou ignored the two and reached for the sealed letter attached to the small door. Written in bold letters across the folded paper were the words: TO MY SONG BIRD.

She looked up at Jack and Alex, feeling tears prick her eyes. "He sent me a bird."

Jack tugged the bedsheet up to her neck. "Please don't drop it in the river as you did the flowers."

Lou shot her a 'be quiet' look. She opened the letter.

My Dearest Lou,
  I love you. It is all I have to say. I pray it is enough.
Fly to me, my little songbird—come home.

                                                          J

Jack moaned. "She has that look again."

"What look?" Alex pulled her hand from the cage.

"That look you had when Captain Matthew Kinkade lay naked on our parlor floor."

"Oh, that look." Alex smiled. "Perhaps we'll see it on you soon enough. I hear Cal is returning soon."

Jack flipped over, giving her back to them. "Don't hold your breath."

Alex made a face at Jack's back and Lou laughed.

"I saw that," Jack murmured.

Alex sat on the edge of Lou's bed. She made kissy noises to the bird, and its red-orange feathers fairly glowed with the attention. "Will you go see him?" she asked, meeting Lou's gaze.

Completely happy, she smiled. Everything was going to be okay. "First thing in the morning."

Concern etched her sister's features. "Take Matt with you. Please."

It seemed as though Lou wasn't the only one who had fears that Hank would return.

"I will."

Alex rose and crossed to the door. "Good night."

After bidding her sister good night, Lou pushed back the covers. She walked to the door, turned the lock, and checked it twice. They she turned down the light and slipped into bed.

Dog continued to ignore him. John sighed. It seemed as though everyone was turning away from him these days.

He stared at the stack of papers on his desk, ready to tackle the pile. At least work would take his mind off Lou. Or at least he hoped it would. Nothing during these last few days had been able to up to this point, despite the many ways he tried to banish her image from his mind.

He hadn't wanted to leave the *Amazing Grace*—or Lou. Especially not with Hank on the loose, but there was little he could do. Lou refused to see him, and he needed to get back to his job. He hoped the promise he elicited from Matt before he left would be enough. Matt swore on his own head that he would watch over Lou and protect her, until she and John could work out their problems.

Picking up a piece of paper, he scanned the page and then set it aside. Outside a cold rain spit against the window. Spring and her fickle heart had turned the tables once again. In his mind, the image of Lou skimming rocks, the sun shining off her hair, appeared.

He savored the memory for a moment before shaking it free. He'd done all he could to explain and make atonement, including sending her a bird. It was up to Lou now to come to him.

Cora came in carrying a small wooden tray laden with a teacup and some biscuits. Dog thumped his tail against the wood floor.

"Seems you made a friend while I was away, Cora."

She smiled, the roundness of her face lifting with the motion. "He'll come round, Reverend." She scratched Dog's ears. "I don't think he thought you'd be coming back."

She cleared her throat. "Not that it's any of my business, but I didn't think you'd be coming back alone."

He crumpled a piece of paper and tossed it on his desk. "To be honest, Cora, neither did I."

"Dare I ask?"

"I'd rather you didn't," he replied, wincing at the memories. "I made quite a fool of myself."

The doorbell chimed and every nerve in John's body jumped to life. Had the canary finally gotten through to Lou?

Cora tsked. "Your heart's fastened to your face. I'll see to the door."

John ran a hand over his hair, smoothing it into place. He straightened his collar and made sure his pants carried no lint.

Cora poked her head through the door. "Mrs. Farrell is here, Reverend. Care to see her?"

John groaned and Dog lifted his head, only to set it back down again. How long was the mutt to be mad at him? It was on the tip of John's tongue to tell Cora to turn the crotchety old woman away, but in the end, he knew duty called.

Rising as Mrs. Farrell entered his study, John offered his welcome. A change had come over her, he noticed immediately. Her face no longer held the sour expression it normally carried; instead, she looked at peace.

Levi Mason was a miracle-worker if he was responsible for the change.

"Please sit down. You look well."

"I am. Quite."

"Does it have anything to do with Levi?"

Her gaze shifted to the floor. "He's helped me to see the person I've become. And I didn't like her." Dog growled, and Mrs. Farrell merely frowned at him rather than poking him with her cane.

"Not many did."

Her eyes widened. "Thank you for that honesty. I'm trying, Reverend, but it's not easy. I've a lifetime of habits to change and wrongs to right."

"There's time enough."

"I hope so." She picked at her fingernails. "I've just now heard of the hunt for Hank Burnett. How terrible for that poor girl."

"She's healing," John said. "On the outside at least."

Coiled curls lay against Mrs. Farrell's forehead, dampened by the rain. Tears puddled in her eyes. "It's all my fault."

"What is?"

"What happened to that girl. I—" Her chin dropped. "I asked Hank to spy on the Parkers. I'm the reason he was on that boat." She looked up quickly. "I never knew the kind of person he was. I never wanted to harm those girls. . . ."

John knew Mrs. Farrell was not responsible for Hank's actions, yet he kept quiet. "That all depends on how you define harm."

"True enough. I deserve harsher words than that." She looked up. "When I was young, I never intended to become a cold-hearted shrew."

"You've known your fair share of hardship."

She nodded, her chins jiggling. "Yes, yes I have. But it is no excuse for my behavior. I have no one to blame but my own self."

"Levi told me of your long-ago engagement to Hiram Parker."

Her eyes rolled. "Our parents arranged the wedding, and I suppose that is where my resentment started to grow. Over the years the resentment turned to anger, then jealousy."

This is a new side to Mrs. Farrell, one he'd never expected to see. "Jealousy?"

"Yes. I never loved Hiram Parker. He was but a friend, and a distant one at that. It was Levi I loved, but my parents refused to hear of a union between us."

John let her continue her story uninterrupted.

"I was nothing but happy when Hiram ran off with Grace Parker. I thought then my parents would allow me to marry Levi. Instead they sent me back East, to a maiden aunt's house, and arranged my marriage to William Farrell."

"Why didn't you just say no?"

"I tried, Reverend, but every time I opened my mouth to fight for what I wanted, I lost all nerve. That's what's been eating me up inside all these years. That I never had the gumption to say what was on my mind, or do what I wanted to do. Hiram ran off with Grace without a backward glance. He then raised his children to be the same way— to speak their minds, to hold their own, to be different and independent. Plain and simple, I envied them with all my might."

Ahhh. So this was the root of Mrs. Farrell's dislike of the Parkers. Now that he knew, he felt remorse for the old woman. He wondered what she'd say if she knew how much she and Lou had in common. Only Lou, thankfully, had been able to change her life course early on, where Mrs. Farrell was just now recognizing the need for change.

"I'm afraid," she continued on, tapping her cane on the floor, "that I took my resentment out on those poor girls. They've never done a thing wrong, and who am I to judge them? If I'd had half the gumption they possess I'd celebrating my thirtieth year as Levi's wife."

God, John was quite sure, had reserved a special spot in heaven for Levi Mason.

"I'm sure they'll understand as soon as you explain yourself to them. They're remarkable women, all three of them."

"About Hank—"

"Hank's doings are his own, Mrs. Farrell. Don't be holding yourself responsible for his actions. You didn't ask him to hurt anyone—"

"Lord, no!"

"Then let it be. Let your conscience be your guide from here on out."

"You mean, now that I can hear it?" she said with a smile. Dog growled and she frowned. "Have to tell you, Reverend, I still don't like that dog."

John laughed. "I believe the feeling is mutual."

Using her cane for leverage, Mrs. Farrell got to her feet. "I wish to apologize for my terrible treatment of you. Please, will you forgive me?"

He pushed out of his chair. "We all make mistakes."

"Will the Miss Parkers be attending services on Sunday?"

"I'm not sure."

A thick eyebrow arched. "Oh?"

He followed her down the hallway and opened the front door. A chill wind swept inside. "As I said, we all make mistakes."

"I do hope things work out."

A week ago he never would have believed her words. Now he sensed there was truth to them. "Thank you. I do too."

"If there's anything I can do to help . . ."

"I'll be sure to ask."

Mrs. Farrell's covered buggy sat in the circular drive. He held an umbrella over her head as she ambled down the walkway. He'd just seen her settled when a horse came galloping up the driveway.

John recognized Jack's dark hair long before he could

see her face. She pulled on the reins, guiding her horse to a stop. She wore a look upon her face that had panic racing through him.

"It's Lou."

Thunder rumbled. Dread laced his words. "What about her?"

"Hank's taken her."

Chapter Sixteen

Pain beat a fierce rhythm in the back of her head. Lou blinked, her eyes strangely unfocused. She was vaguely aware of the wind and rain as a storm raged outside.

Where was she?

She tried to sit up, but something held her down. She called out to Jack, and was horrified to find something blocking her mouth.

Cloth. She'd been gagged. Wiggling her fingers, she found that her hands had been tied together, as had her feet. Fear rolled over her.

"Stop wiggling."

A face hovered above her. Hollow eyes raked over her and she fought rising panic.

Hank!

How? How had this come about? In the blink of an eye, she remembered.

"Mmmmmtttt," she said through the thick cloth. Matt. She'd been with him, on her way to see John. They'd been walking along the Public Landing, headed for the livery, when she'd heard a commotion behind her. She'd turned to find Matt on the ground, his head bleeding. She'd bent over him. . . . And that was all she recalled.

Hank must have been waiting on the Landing, blending in with the riffraff, just waiting for the opportunity to kidnap her.

"Mmmmmtttt," she said again. There had been much blood staining the cobblestones. She prayed Matt was okay, that someone had come to his aid. How would Alex go on otherwise?

Hank peered down at her. "Stop. Talking." He turned away.

Blinking back tears, she wondered how she had ever thought him a kind, simple man. His eyes held evil.

What would he do with her? She thought of Daphne and shuddered.

She stared up at the ceiling, willing herself not to cry. It was a weakness, her father often said, and she didn't want to show Hank how he frightened her. She called on every ounce of courage she possessed to calm herself. With effort, her tremors subsided.

She looked around at her surroundings. She couldn't see much due to her confines, but what she saw scared her all the more. Split logs framed the room, and to her eye, it seemed as though that was all it was. One room. His fishing cabin?

To her right, she heard the unmistakable sound of metal upon metal as Hank sharpened a knife.

Breathing deeply through her nose, she fought to retain her composure. If she panicked now, all would be lost. Surely there was a way for her to escape, to use some of the skills her father had taught her.

She tried not to flinch every time his blade struck steel. Grateful for the cover, she worked the bindings on her hands, timing the rustling to coincide with the rhythmic sharpening of the knife.

From the corner of her eye she could see Hank, his back to her.

She'd nearly worked the bindings loose enough for her hands to slip through when Hank stood.

Knife in hand, he walked toward her, his blade at the ready. He raised back his hand, knife shining, and slashed it downward.

Her scream split the air as her gag fell free.

His laughter pulsed around the room. "Didn't think I'd let you die so easily, did you?"

Her heart slammed against her breastbone. Her breathing came quick and shallow. Her knees shook.

Hank trailed the knife loosely down her cheek, her chin, her neck.

She swallowed hard and gasped as she felt the tip of the cold metal prick her skin just above her collarbone.

"Now look what you've gone and done." He studied the drop of blood on the blade. "Now I have to clean it." He turned away.

Unintentionally, she had garnered herself time. Time she desperately needed to plot, to plan. Time, perhaps, others could use trying to find her.

It could be her only hope.

"He could be anywhere," Alex cried.

Absently, John watched as Matt wrapped an arm around her and pulled her close. A cloth, now soaked in blood, had been tied around Matt's head.

Rain beat against the stained glass windows of the church. Candlelight glowed on the faces surrounding him. Familiar faces such as those of Levi, Mrs. Farrell, Hex Goolens, and his gaggle of siblings. Hannah O'Grady and her young son too. All had come running when they heard the news of Lou's abduction, and it warmed his heart to see the change in his congregation, but worry of Lou's safety overrode all other feelings at the moment.

"His home has been searched?" John asked.

"He stays with his ma and pa," Levi said, "who swear they haven't seen nor heard from him in weeks."

John's eyes narrowed on the old man's face. "Do you believe them?"

He shrugged. "I'm inclined to, but I've been known to be wrong afore."

John rubbed his hand over his face, letting his eyes drift closed for a moment. Time seemed to be rushing by. What had Hank done to her? Was she all right? Did she know they were all looking for her? Did she realize how much he cared?

His legs wobbled just a bit, and he lowered himself into a pew. Dog placed his head on his lap.

She had been coming to see him when Hank took her. To reconcile? To tell him to leave her be? He didn't know. He pushed aside the thought that he might never know. He refused to believe it, or to even entertain the notion.

He would get her back.

Surging to his feet, he glanced at the map of the area. "Hank has to be at a place he feels safe. He wouldn't dare take her on the run with half the law in the country searching him out. Where?"

Jack's head snapped up, her eyes red-rimmed. She snapped her fingers. "Hank brought her trout once."

Alex gasped. "Lou mentioned to Matthew and me that Hank had invited her fishing. Said he had a small cabin."

"Where?" John asked.

Shaking her head, Alex sighed. "I don't know. She didn't say."

"Jack?"

"No, Reverend. I don't know either."

"Do any of you know where Hank's fishing cabin is?" Horror filled him as each person looked away.

"I might know."

John spun. "Where, Mrs. Farrell?"

She hesitated.

Jack cried, "Please, if you know, you must tell us. Lou is in terrible danger."

The color drained from Mrs. Farrell's face. "My interest is to see Lou returned safe and sound, Miss Parker. I hesitate only because my mind isn't once what it was. I must go to the bank and check my records." She turned on her heel, her cane punctuating her hasty exit.

The air grew thick with tension as they waited for Mrs. Farrell to return. Alex brushed past John, taking a seat on the pew beside him. "She'll be okay, John."

"I feel so helpless."

"She's strong. And brave."

It was true. If anyone could outwit Hank, it was Lou. But she was such a tiny thing, would Hank simply overpower her? Thinking of Daphne, his heart clenched. Was Lou hurt?

"Is Matt okay?"

Alex glanced over her shoulder at Matt as he studied the maps. "He's angry, John. So angry. I'm a bit worried about him."

Since rage simmered beneath John's skin, he knew exactly how Matt felt. "We need to find Hank."

He jumped as the church's double doors swung open. Rain splashed on the wooden floors as Mrs. Farrell hobbled in, a piece of paper held high in a triumphant hand. "I recalled I sold Hank a plot of land a while back. I didn't know he'd built anything on it."

John rushed down the aisle and took the paper. It specified the exact location. He looked to Matt. "Ready?"

Matt's lips were set in a hard line. "More than ready, Reverend."

They spent a few minutes talking the rest of the group out of accompanying them out to Hank's shanty. John counted on a surprise attack to catch Hank, and that wasn't possible with the whole town galloping in with them.

Jack's eyes blazed. "I'm coming."

Reluctantly, John nodded.

"Alex, are you coming?" Jack asked.

Matt held her tightly, whispering in her ear, and she pressed a protective hand to her stomach. Tears seeped from her eyes. "No."

Jack seemed to come to the same realization as John. She rushed to Alex's side and took her hand. "Are you. . . ." She gestured downward.

Slowly, Alex nodded, a small smile tilting her lips.

Jack turned on her heel and faced John. "I'm staying with Alex."

Alex crossed to John and kissed his cheek. "Bring her back."

"I plan to."

Rain soaked him through as he reached his horse and swung into the saddle. He reached behind him, removed the white collar from around his neck, and stuffed it into his pocket.

He didn't want to be wearing it when he killed Hank Burnett.

Chapter Seventeen

She'd just about worked her hands free. A few more wiggles and a twist to the right . . .

Yes!

Hank turned, casting a sharp gaze toward her, and she froze, forcing innocence into her eyes.

"This wouldn't be happening," he snarled, "if you had chosen me over him."

Him. John.

A lump settled in her throat, choking her. She'd never had the chance to apologize, to make things right. Did he know how much she loved him?

"He is—" She broke off. Did she really want to rile Hank further by defending John?

In two quick strides, Hank crossed the room and grabbed a fistful of her blouse. She forced herself to bite her tongue to keep from saying something that would get her into deeper trouble.

"What were you saying?"

The coppery taste of blood greeted her tongue as she wet her lips. She straightened her shoulders and lifted her chin. "I said John is one hundred times the man you'll ever be."

Hank flexed his fingers and the shoulder seam of her blouse ripped as he pulled her forward. He stared at her long and hard, and though she wanted to look away from those empty, soulless eyes, she didn't. Abruptly, he released her.

Rain leaked through the ceiling, dripping onto the earthen floor with a steady splash. She focused on the puddle being made instead of on Hank.

He walked away. Picking up his knife, he tested the point on his thumb, drawing blood, then laid the knife back on the table. He turned to her. Menace dripped from his lips as he spoke. "The good reverend ain't as saintly as he'd have people believe."

Her temper flared white-hot. "Someone the likes of you shouldn't be making saintly comparisons."

He raised his hand, and she stared straight into his bottomless eyes. If she were going to die by his hand, she would die with honor.

"Is that so?"

She kept quiet, not liking the way he spoke with his words slurring. His control was weakening, and that was the last thing she wanted. She had yet to formulate a plan of escape.

She tested the bindings on her wrists. Still loose. She just needed to time the precise moment to make her move.

"Then why was the good reverend aboard the *Amazing Grace*?" he asked, still staring at the opening in her blouse.

His lecherous glare made her want to claw his face. Tightly, she said, "Perhaps he needed a vacation."

He laughed, and the jarring noise grated on her taut nerves.

What was his point? She'd never really considered why John had been aboard the *Amazing Grace*. She'd assumed he'd been there to see her. Had she been wrong?

"Really? Then I'd like to know why Mrs. Farrell paid his fare."

Mrs. Farrell? Why would she have paid for John's ticket?

"I'd always heard you was an apple shy of the bushel. You fell for that goody boy without even thinking about what he'd want from you."

Her head pounded, and her mouth ached as she drew in a deep breath. Using the calming noise of the rainwater, she struggled to find the courage she needed to get out of this cabin alive.

It took all her might not to comment on his perception of her. Her gaze skipped from the widening puddle on the floor to him knife lying on the log table by the door.

"Simple-minded Lou. Pretty to look at, but not much in the way of thinking. How's it feel to know he conned you? Raked you over and left you hung out to dry?"

She'd brought this on herself, all those years she'd kept her opinions to herself, she realized. She fought the urge to lash out. Let him keep talking, she told herself. She wanted him to think she was simple. It could only aid in her escape.

"Perhaps," she said tightly, "he was short on funds."

Crossing his arms over his chest, Hank rocked on his heels, sending the water in the puddle rippling across the floor. "I know for a fact that Mrs. Farrell bought the reverend's agreement to spy on you. To get hisself close to you to learn information that would get you kicked out of town for good."

She schooled her features so as not to show her shock. John wouldn't. He was too honorable. . . .

Wasn't he?

Doubt wiggled in, burrowing into her thoughts. He had kept his past a secret from her, but that had all been explained.

However, Mrs. Farrell's interference would explain

John's sudden appearance on the *Amazing Grace*. She just couldn't believe it.

She recalled his words that day they spent at the river's edge:

There is nothing about you not to care for . . . not to love. You must know by now that I love you, Lou. I love your temper, your zest for life. I love that you know how to swing a baseball bat, and I even love that you can't cook but still you try.

No. For whatever reason John had been aboard, he'd never betray what they shared. Of that she was certain.

"And how might you know of this, Hank?"

Wolfishly, he grinned, revealing long, fang-like teeth. "I know, cuz she hired me too."

It all fell into place. How Hank always seemed to follow her about, how he came looking for a job out of the blue, and how Mrs. Farrell knew of the happenings aboard the *Amazing Grace*.

Thunder boomed overhead, shaking the walls of the cabin. "What do you think of your good reverend now?"

Part of her wished she could break the vow she'd made to herself and go back to being manipulative. Easily, she could bat her eyelashes, pout, and simper in order to trick Hank. She could deny her feelings for John and possibly be freed. . . .

And once again become a woman with no principles. She'd laid *that* Lou Parker to rest. Forever. The new Lou fought for what she believed in and stood her ground, no matter the consequences.

Her chin tilted upward. "I love John Hewitt. Now and always, and nothing you can say about him will change that. Ever."

She anticipated his attack, and when he lunged, she lurched, pressing her head into his stomach.

She rolled to the side as he jerked back in surprise, wheezing.

Pulling her hands free, she held onto her determination to escape . . . and to see John again.

With a quick jab, she poked Hank in the eyes, temporarily blinding him. She hopped over to the door, muddy water splashing her ankles, thankful once again that she was wearing pants.

He howled and stumbled about the room as if in a drunken stupor, and she moved quickly.

She grabbed his knife from the table, and a quick flick of her wrist had her legs free.

Hank grabbed her from behind. She drove the knife deep into his leg, and slammed her elbow into his gut.

His hold loosened as he cursed her a blue streak. She spun and kicked him below the belt.

His yowl of pain ricocheted from wall to wall. Lou fumbled with the latch on the door and stumbled into the rain. Lightning split the darkening sky. She went with instinct and turned right, into the woods behind the cabin.

Rain pelted her face. Her breaths echoed in her ears. Behind her she heard Hank grunt as he followed her footsteps.

Pain pulsed behind her eyes with each step she took. Twigs snapped as she ran farther into the woods, past moss-encrusted tree trunks, and toward the darkness.

Her ankle rolled as she stepped on a stone, and she fell. The air whooshed from her lungs, and it took a precious moment to regain her feet.

Blood trickled from her scraped palms as she looked over her shoulder. Hank was but fifty feet away, his grin an eerie glow in the falling night.

She froze.

"You can run, but I can catch you."

Quickly, she bent down and grabbed the rock she

had tripped over. Rounded, it was smooth, damp, and cool to the touch.

The overhead branches shielded her from most of the rain, but Lou was already soaked through. Her fist tightened, lest the rock slip from her hand.

He stepped closer, his movements surprisingly limber. Blood leaked from the hole in his pants, dripping down his leg.

She settled the rock in her palm as he inched nearer. Taking a deep breath, she twirled her arm once, twice. She stepped forward on the third rotation and let the rock fly.

Hank fell with a thud, a small dark spot of blood marring his forehead where the rock hit.

"You're out," she muttered under her breath.

The gray of the day turned darker yet, and Lou realized night was falling quickly.

She had no idea where she was or how far away from home. The idea of running deeper into the wild filled her with apprehension. When lost, her father had often said, stay put.

She distanced herself from Hank, but chose a tree where she could still see his body. Shimmying up the trunk of an old red maple, she nestled herself high above the ground, out of sight. Heaving a deep sigh, she counted her many blessings, and let her head fall back against the bark.

Minutes later, her head snapped up as a twig cracked. Her gaze shot to Hank, a dark lump on the forest floor, and she briefly wondered if it was possible she'd killed him.

Her head jerked right. Another snap. Dusky light filtered in from above. Every shadow seemed alive.

Goose bumps raised on her arms. One of the shadows moved, and Lou thought she was seeing things until she made out the outline of a man dressed all in black. He crept from tree to tree.

Her first thought was that John had found her, but as he

neared, she saw that he wore no white collar, for it would have been a beacon of hope in the gloomy night.

Rain spit from the sky, a lazy drizzle. The man suddenly straightened. With cautious steps, his arms outstretched, he crept toward Hank.

After a moment, he bent down and felt Hank's neck, then rose again. He looked all around, called something out she couldn't quite hear, and took a step toward the tree in which she hid.

She strained her eyes. It couldn't be, could it? Her heart skipped a beat as it pulsed against her ribs.

She knew that profile, that gait.

"John?"

Her voice came out as a mere croak, yet his head snapped in her direction.

"Lou?" All around her, birds flew from their nests.

"Up here." She surged forward and quickly grabbed a branch before she tumbled twenty feet to the ground.

He glanced up, his teeth shining in the night. "Are you all right?"

"I am now that you're here."

She came down another branch, her foot slipping on the slick bark. Looking down at him, her stomach twisted in a painful knot. She was so incredibly thankful to see him again.

A shadow lurched, catching her eye.

"John!" she screamed.

John spun and caught Hank's wrist just as he was about to bring a rock down on his head.

Lou scrambled down the tree, the bark tearing at her skin. She watched in horror as John and Hank struggled.

Hank broke free of John's grasp and threw a punch that had John doubling over. Once bent at the waist, John grabbed Hank's feet out from under him. Hank groaned as he hit the ground. John hauled him to his feet and hit him once, twice, three times. Hank bellowed and kicked out, knocking John to the ground.

Lou screamed and plunged forward. Her arms flapped like a bird as she fell. She bounced on a branch, and was abruptly yanked to a halt when her pants snagged on a dead limb.

Beneath her, John kicked upward and Hank stumbled back.

Matt's voice came out of the darkness. "Don't move or I'll be forced to pull this trigger. It will upset my wife to no end if I am forced to kill you. You okay, Reverend?"

"Took you long enough to get here."

"It's dark out here." There was humor in Matt's voice.

Lou watched from above as Matt pushed a gun into John's hands. For a brief second she thought she could sense John's desire to use the weapon.

Matt secured Hank's hands and feet with rope and pushed him to the ground. John handed the gun back.

"Lou?" Matt called out. "You okay?"

"I'm fine."

"You can come down now," John said.

"Wish I could."

John looked up, a smile etching his handsome face. The branch holding her cracked, and Lou let out a shriek as she plummeted downward.

John held open his arms as she crashed through the foliage. Her weight knocked him to the ground.

He ran his hands over her back, her shoulders, her face. His fingers lingered on the small cut on her lip. "I'm going to kill him."

"No." She pressed her cheek into his palm. "Let God decide his punishment. Until then, let him rot in prison."

"I love you," he said.

"I love you, John. So much."

He held her close, his heart beating against her breastbone. "Funny how we keep meeting like this," he whispered against her neck, his warm breath sending chills up her spine.

Lou sought his lips in the darkness. Raindrops rolled down her face as she kissed him, reveling in all she had almost lost.

Matt's voice cut through the darkness. "Save it for the wedding night, you two. We've a whole town waiting on us."

"A wedding sounds like a mighty fine idea, don't you agree?"

She searched John's eyes, seeing the love he had for her. "Absolutely. A wedding," she said, already dreaming of the day. And night . . . "As soon as possible?"

A smile lit his whole face, lighting his eyes. "I think that can be arranged."

He kissed her gently, his lips holding a promise of what was to come.

"You're cold," he said, noticing she was shivering. "Come on." He tugged her to her feet. "Let's get you warm."

"Actually," she said, smiling, "you were doing a fine job of that right where we were."

He laughed. "Thank God you're okay."

She stumbled over a rock and John's strong hand kept her from falling. "Eloisa told me of your father. She told me a lot of things, really. I wish you had told me."

"I would have, given time."

She tugged John to a stop. "Will you go see him?"

He cupped her face. "I don't know if I can."

"I'm not able to make reparations with my father, and I shall regret it till the day I die. Don't let it happen to you too."

Her rested his forehead on the top of her head. "I can try. It's all I can promise."

She smiled. "It's all I hoped for. Perhaps we can journey to New York for our wedding trip?"

He nodded in the darkness. "Let's go home."

He held her close as he led her through the forest, trailing Matt. Lou looked up at him. "What did Matt mean by a whole town was waiting for us?"

"River Glen." John wrapped his arm around her shoulder. "They all helped in finding you."

She looked up at him. The night shadowed his face, but she could still make out his features. "Why?"

"Because they care."

They cared. Tears spilled from her eyes and mixed with the raindrops.

"It'll be okay," he soothed.

Only it wouldn't. Because now she had to admit to all the people who helped find her—who cared for her—that she was Madame Angelique.

What would they think of her then?

"About that wedding?" John asked.

Worry still lingered, but the happiness in knowing that John would soon be her husband buoyed her spirit. "Yes?"

"How soon is soon?"

She smiled.

Chapter Eighteen

Eloisa stared critically at Lou's face.

"What?" Lou asked, turning toward the mirror. "Do I look like a circus clown?"

Dog thumped his tail. He hadn't left her side since she, along with Daphne, moved into John's house a week ago.

"No." Eloisa put a finger to her lip in contemplation. "Perhaps . . ." She reached for the powder on the vanity.

Lou peered at her reflection. "It looks okay to me. Let's let Daphne be the judge." Turning on the small bench, Lou gave her attention to the young woman sitting up in bed, pillows bunched behind her. "Daphne?"

With each daily trip to John's house, Doc Steiner assured them all that Daphne was fit as a fiddle and would be up in no time. The knock she had taken to her head when she'd fallen had caused a concussion, and Daphne had been plagued with headaches and dizziness ever since. John had invited her to stay at his house until she was completely well, and Eloisa had postponed her return trip to New York and volunteered to help take care of her. "I think you look wonderful, but then you always do, whether you're dressed as Madame Angelique or just being you."

Eloisa came up behind her and twirled a lock of the copper wig that hid Lou's blond hair. "I agree."

Lou's eyes welled. She rose quickly, nearly tripping in the shoes with the high wedges, and kissed Daphne's cheek. "Thank you."

A tear rolled from Lou's eye. Hastily, she wiped it away before it ruined all Eloisa's handiwork. She stood and kissed the older woman's cheek. "Family *is* what's most important. I will try to remember that when I'm singing before the whole town and they're sneering at me," she said with a wry smile.

Daphne tossed a pillow at Lou. "Stop that nonsense. They will love you, just as all of us do."

"Amen."

Lou spun around at the sound of John's voice. He stood framed in the large doorway, leaning against the jamb. His collar hung loose, and his buttons were undone.

Lou smiled. She carefully crossed the room, trying to keep her balance. Dog kept step with her every move. John tugged her into the hall, closed the door to Daphne's bedroom, and kissed her soundly.

Longing, and a hunger that had yet to be satiated, flowed through her. She reached up and ran her hands through his hair, and loved that she had every right to do so.

Pressing her closer to the wall, he deepened the kiss, sending her senses soaring. Abruptly, he pulled back, leaving her wanting more.

"If we continue that, we'll be late."

"That was my intention," she teased.

Kissing the tip of her nose, he said, "Second thoughts about the concert?"

"And thirds and fourths." She had been the one to come up with the plan to give a concert for the people of River Glen to reveal Madame Angelique's true identity. The gazebo behind the church had been readied for her performance, and word had gone out that John had a special surprise for the town. Fear had taken root in her stomach days ago and she felt slightly ill.

"You will be wonderful."

She fell into his embrace, loving how her head fit neatly into the crook of his neck, thanks to Madame Angelique's shoes. "Thank you for allowing me to do this."

"I never asked you to give up your job as Madame Angelique." He nudged up her chin and looked her in the eye. Bright blue orbs stared at her intently. "To do so would clip your wings . . . and your dreams would then die. I could never let that happen."

Pulling out his watch, he frowned at what he saw. "We must go."

She buttoned the top two buttons on his black shirt, letting her fingers trail against his skin as she did so. She looked up at him with a coquettish smile and loved the blatant desire in his eyes. "Let me just say my good-byes to Daphne, and I'll be right down."

"You better go quickly," he said through clenched teeth, his hands skimming her waist.

As she reluctantly pulled away, he caught her arm. "No matter what happens, remember I love you."

"Always."

It was Levi who introduced her.

"Reverend Hewitt wanted to give all us a special treat this fine afternoon. Him thinkin' we deserved one, fer no reason I can gather."

Behind the curtains shading the gazebo, Lou shuddered. What if they booed her? Threw things? Her lips ached from being bitten so hard. Would she be able to sing once she revealed herself? Or would her voice fail her?

Silent questions bombarded her, and she barely caught Levi's cue.

"Straight from the *Amazing Grace*, this here's Madame Angelique."

Lou sucked in a breath, fear paralyzing her as the curtains swung open. A murmur rolled through the crowd as the light from the spring day spilled across her.

With a tinge of horror, she watched as Mrs. Beasley covered little Tommy's eyes.

She shot a look to John, who stood with her family. He smiled in encouragement, and Jack made a talking motion with her hand.

With a start, Lou began to sing. The words to the love song spilled from her soul, and she barely took her eyes from John as she sang.

When she did look around, she found Mrs. Beasley's frown turning to a smile, and little Tommy gawking as his mother released her blindfold of fingers. Levi had his hands crossed over his chest and a smirk on his face. She winked at him and enjoyed the color rising like a swift tide up his cheeks.

Mrs. Farrell sat in a chair dragged out of the schoolhouse, and she appeared to have had lemons for lunch. Her lips were pursed, her face pinched into a tight frown.

How shocked she would be when she learned it was Lou behind the mask, but perhaps not as shocked as Lou had been when Mrs. Farrell had sought her out and asked her forgiveness earlier in the week.

Notes soared upward into the sky as she finished the chorus and launched into the final refrain.

Though she and Mrs. Farrell might not ever be the closest of friends, they'd formed a truce. Or at least they had until today.

Butterflies circled her stomach, but the notes stayed strong as she sang. With a long look at John, she ended the song. Without giving time for a response from those gathered, she launched into her next song, the one with which she always closed her show.

From deep within, she gave all she had and put it into the words of the hymn.

Amazing Grace! How sweet the sound . . .

Her smoky voice seemed to have captivated all who had gathered, for most of them stared open-mouthed at her.

She looked to John. *'Twas grace that taught my heart to fear, And grace my fears relieved.*

Without him, his encouragement and love, she couldn't have done this. Oh, how she loved him. *His* grace, his integrity, his honor.

She slipped the wig off her head; let it fall to the floor in a copper puddle.

Through many dangers, toils and snares, I have already come, 'Tis grace hath brought me safe this far . . .

She looked to Mrs. Farrell.

And grace will lead me home.

Her gaze shifted. Hex Goolens wore the biggest grin she'd ever seen, and she waved at him.

She reached for the mask. Her hand shook. Her voice wavered. *I shall possess within the veil, a life of joy and peace. When we've been there ten thousand year . . .*

She tugged the mask over her head, and those who hadn't recognized her hair, gasped.

Fully exposed as herself, she wondered for the briefest of seconds whether her voice would fail. Full of doubt, she sought John in the crowd. He flapped his arms like a chicken, and she nearly laughed out loud, yet she knew his meaning.

Fly.

She opened her mouth, and called upon every ounce of grace *she* possessed. *We've no less days to sing God's praise . . .*

She paused and smiled as the final notes rang out.

As when we've first begun.

John appeared at her side and took hold of her hand. "Friends," he called out, his voice washing over the crowd, "I'd like to introduce you to Madame Angelique." He turned, looked at her, and pulled her close. "My wife, Lou Hewitt."

Lou shuddered as a gasp rolled through the crowd, yet with John's arms holding her tight, she remembered how much love she had. For a week, since the night John found her in the forest, she'd been his wife, and loved hearing him call her so.

Each second of silence resonated like the toll of a death bell. Her bottom lip quavered and she bit it. Her chin lifted upward as John looked at her, compassion shining in his eyes.

Her voice cracked. "Let's go home."

She turned to go, and froze as one person clapped. Then another clapped. Looking out over the crowd, she saw Hex Goolens clapping like a fool. To her right, Levi Mason had joined in. She watched in amazement as one by one, the townspeople got to their feet and started cheering.

Tears sprang to Lou's eyes. John kissed her tenderly before taking a step back and presenting her with his arms wide. Applause echoed across the open field, and even Mrs. Farrell rose to her feet, though she did not clap until Levi nudged her with his elbow.

Lou heard a whistle in the rear and recognized it as Jack's. She bowed to the crowd, tears streaming down her face.

John wrapped his arms around her. "How does it feel," he whispered, "to be free of your cage?"

She cupped his face with her hands and kissed his lips. "Amazing."

And looking out over the cheering crowd, she thought that being honest had never felt so good.

JUL   2003